Shooting an Elephant

Other books by George Orwell

Shooting an Elephant

AND OTHER ESSAYS

by George Orwell

Harcourt Brace Jovanovich, Publishers
San Diego   New York   London

These essays have appeared in the following magazines:
*New Writing, Horizon, The Adelphi, Now, Polemic,
Tribune, The New Republic*, and *Partisan Review*.

ISBN 0-15-182043-0
PRINTED IN THE UNITED STATES OF AMERICA

HIJKLMNO

Editor's Note

THE FIRST THREE OF THESE ESSAYS WERE WRITTEN BETWEEN 1931 and 1936, the rest between 1945 and 1949. The pieces grouped together under the title "I Write as I Please" are a selection from a weekly column which George Orwell wrote for the British magazine, *Tribune.* Written under these conditions they cannot be considered in the same category as the other essays and have been included because of their charm and because they express ideas which he has not developed elsewhere.

Contents

Shooting an Elephant

Shooting an Elephant

IN MOULMEIN, IN LOWER BURMA, I WAS HATED BY LARGE NUM-
bers.of people—the only time in my life that I have been
important enough for this to happen to me. I was sub-divi-
sional police officer of the town, and in an aimless, petty kind
of way anti-European feeling was very bitter. No one had the
guts to raise a riot, but if a European woman went through
the bazaars alone somebody would probably spit betel juice
over her dress. As a police officer I was an obvious target and
was baited whenever it seemed safe to do so. When a nimble
Burman tripped me up on the football field and the referee
(another Burman) looked the other way, the crowd yelled with
hideous laughter. This happened more than once. In the end
the sneering yellow faces of young men that met me everywhere, the insults hooted after me when I was at a safe distance, got badly on my nerves. The young Buddhist priests
were the worst of all. There were several thousands of them
in the town and none of them seemed to have anything to
do except stand on street corners and jeer at Europeans.

All this was perplexing and upsetting. For at that time I
had already made up my mind that imperialism was an evil
thing and the sooner I chucked up my job and got out of it
the better. Theoretically—and secretly, of course—I was all
for the Burmese and all against their oppressors, the British.
As for the job I was doing, I hated it more bitterly than I can

perhaps make clear. In a job like that you see the dirty work of Empire at close quarters. The wretched prisoners huddling in the stinking cages of the lock-ups, the grey, cowed faces of the long-term convicts, the scarred buttocks of the men who had been flogged with bamboos—all these oppressed me with an intolerable sense of guilt. But I could get nothing into perspective. I was young and ill-educated and I had had to think out my problems in the utter silence that is imposed on every Englishman in the East. I did not even know that the British Empire is dying, still less did I know that it is a great deal better than the younger empires that are going to supplant it. All I knew was that I was stuck between my hatred of the empire I served and my rage against the evil-spirited little beasts who tried to make my job impossible. With one part of my mind I thought of the British Raj as an unbreakable tyranny, as something clamped down, in *saecula saeculorum,* upon the will of prostrate peoples; with another part I thought that the greatest joy in the world would be to drive a bayonet into a Buddhist priest's guts. Feelings like these are the normal by-products of imperialism; ask any Anglo-Indian official, if you can catch him off duty.

One day something happened which in a roundabout way was enlightening. It was a tiny incident in itself, but it gave me a better glimpse than I had had before of the real nature of imperialism—the real motives for which despotic governments act. Early one morning the sub-inspector at a police station the other end of the town rang me up on the 'phone and said that an elephant was ravaging the bazaar. Would I please come and do something about it? I did not know what I could do, but I wanted to see what was happening and I got on to a pony and started out. I took my rifle, an old .44 Winchester and much too small to kill an elephant, but I thought the noise might be useful *in terrorem.* Various Burmans stopped me on the way and told me about the elephant's doings. It was not, of course, a wild elephant, but a tame one which had gone "must." It had been chained up, as tame elephants always are when their attack of "must" is due, but on the previous night it had broken its chain and escaped. Its mahout, the only person who could manage it when it was in that state, had set out in pursuit, but had taken the wrong direction and was now twelve hours' journey away, and in the morning the elephant had suddenly reappeared in the town. The Burmese population had no weapons and were quite helpless against it. It had already destroyed somebody's bamboo hut, killed a cow and raided some fruit-stalls and devoured the stock; also it had met the municipal rubbish van and, when the driver jumped out and took to his heels, had turned the van over and inflicted violences upon it.

The Burmese sub-inspector and some Indian constables were waiting for me in the quarter where the elephant had been seen. It was a very poor quarter, a labyrinth of squalid bamboo huts, thatched with palm-leaf, winding all over a steep hillside. I remember that it was a cloudy, stuffy morning at the beginning of the rains. We began questioning the people as to where the elephant had gone and, as usual, failed to get any definite information. That is invariably the case in the East; a story always sounds clear enough at a distance, but the nearer you get to the scene of events the vaguer it becomes. Some of the people said that the elephant had gone in one direction, some said that he had gone in another, some professed not even to have heard of any elephant. I had almost made up my mind that the whole story was a pack of lies, when we heard yells a little distance away. There was a loud, scandalized cry of "Go away, child! Go away this instant!" and an old woman with a switch in her hand came round the corner of a hut, violently shooing away a crowd of naked children. Some more women followed, clicking their tongues and exclaiming; evidently there was something that the children ought not to have seen. I rounded the hut and saw a man's dead body sprawling in the mud. He was an Indian, a black Dravidian coolie, almost naked, and he could not have been dead many minutes. The people said that the elephant had come suddenly upon him round the corner of the hut, caught him with its trunk, put its foot on his back and ground him into the earth. This was the rainy season and the ground was soft, and his face had scored a trench a foot deep and a couple of yards long. He was lying on his belly with arms crucified and head sharply twisted to one side. His face was coated with mud, the eyes wide open, the teeth bared and grinning with an expression of unendurable agony. (Never tell me, by the way, that the dead look peaceful. Most of the corpses I have seen looked devilish.) The friction of the great beast's foot had stripped the skin from his back as neatly as one skins a rabbit. As soon as I saw the dead man I sent an orderly to a friend's house nearby to borrow an elephant rifle. I had already sent back the pony, not wanting it to go mad with fright and throw me if it smelt the elephant.

The orderly came back in a few minutes with a rifle and five cartridges, and meanwhile some Burmans had arrived and told us that the elephant was in the paddy fields below, only a few hundred yards away. As I started forward practically the whole population of the quarter flocked out of the houses and followed me. They had seen the rifle and were all shouting excitedly that I was going to shoot the elephant. They had not shown much interest in the elephant when he was merely ravaging their homes, but it was different now that he was going to be shot. It was a bit of fun to them, as it would be to an English crowd; besides they wanted the meat. It made me vaguely uneasy. I had no intention of shooting the elephant

—I had merely sent for the rifle to defend myself if necessary —and it is always unnerving to have a crowd following you. I marched down the hill, looking and feeling a fool, with the rifle over my shoulder and an ever-growing army of people jostling at my heels. At the bottom, when you got away from the huts, there was a metalled road and beyond that a miry waste of paddy fields a thousand yards across, not yet ploughed but soggy from the first rains and dotted with coarse grass. The elephant was standing eight yards from the road, his left side towards us. He took not the slightest notice of the crowd's approach. He was tearing up bunches of grass, beating them against his knees to clean them and stuffing them into his mouth.

I had halted on the road. As soon as I saw the elephant I knew with perfect certainty that I ought not to shoot him. It is a serious matter to shoot a working elephant—it is comparable to destroying a huge and costly piece of machinery— and obviously one ought not to do it if it can possibly be avoided. And at that distance, peacefully eating, the elephant looked no more dangerous than a cow. I thought then and I think now that his attack of "must" was already passing off; in which case he would merely wander harmlessly about until the mahout came back and caught him. Moreover, I did not in the least want to shoot him. I decided that I would watch him for a little while to make sure that he did not turn savage again, and then go home.

But at that moment I glanced round at the crowd that had followed me. It was an immense crowd, two thousand at the least and growing every minute. It blocked the road for a long distance on either side. I looked at the sea of yellow faces above the garish clothes—faces all happy and excited over this bit of fun, all certain that the elephant was going to be shot. They were watching me as they would watch a conjurer about to perform a trick. They did not like me, but with the magical rifle in my hands I was momentarily worth watching. And suddenly I realized that I should have to shoot the elephant after all. The people expected it of me and I had got to do it; I could feel their two thousand wills pressing me forward, irresistibly. And it was at this moment, as I stood there with the rifle in my hands, that I first grasped the hollowness, the futility of the white man's dominion in the East. Here was I, the white man with his gun, standing in front of the unarmed native crowd—seemingly the leading actor of the piece; but in reality I was only an absurd puppet pushed to and fro by the will of those yellow faces behind. I perceived in this moment that when the white man turns tyrant it is his own freedom that he destroys. He becomes a sort of hollow, posing dummy, the conventionalized figure of a sahib. For it is the condition of his rule that he shall spend his life in trying to impress the "natives," and so in every crisis he has got to do what the "natives" expect of him. He wears a mask, and his face grows to fit it. I had got to shoot the elephant. I had committed myself to doing it when I sent for the rifle. A sahib has got to act like a sahib; he has got to appear resolute, to know his own mind and do definite things. To come all that way, rifle in hand, with two thousand people marching at my heels, and then to trail feebly away, having done nothing—no, that was impossible. The crowd would laugh at me. And my whole life, every white man's life in the East, was one long struggle not to be laughed at.

But I did not want to shoot the elephant. I watched him beating his bunch of grass against his knees, with that preoccupied grandmotherly air that elephants have. It seemed to me that it would be murder to shoot him. At that age I was not squeamish about killing animals, but I had never shot an elephant and never wanted to. (Somehow it always seems

worse to kill a *large* animal.) Besides, there was the beast's
owner to be considered. Alive, the elephant was worth at least
a hundred pounds; dead, he would only be worth the value of
his tusks, five pounds, possibly. But I had got to act quickly.
I turned to some experienced-looking Burmans who had been
there when we arrived, and asked them how the elephant had
been behaving. They all said the same thing: he took no
notice of you if you left him alone, but he might charge if you
went too close to him.

It was perfectly clear to me what I ought to do. I ought to
walk up to within, say, twenty-five yards of the elephant and
test his behavior. If he charged, I could shoot; if he took no
notice of me, it would be safe to leave him until the mahout
came back. But also I knew that I was going to do no such
thing. I was a poor shot with a rifle and the ground was soft
mud into which one would sink at every step. If the elephant
charged and I missed him, I should have about as much chance
as a toad under a steam-roller. But even then I was not thinking particularly of my own skin, only of the watchful yellow
faces behind. For at that moment, with the crowd watching
me, I was not afraid in the ordinary sense, as I would have
been if I had been alone. A white man mustn't be frightened
in front of "natives"; and so, in general, he isn't frightened.
The sole thought in my mind was that if anything went wrong
those two thousand Burmans would see me pursued, caught,
trampled on and reduced to a grinning corpse like that Indian
up the hill. And if that happened it was quite probable that
some of them would laugh. That would never do. There was
only one alternative. I shoved the cartridges into the magazine and lay down on the road to get a better aim.

The crowd grew very still, and a deep, low, happy sigh, as
of people who see the theatre curtain go up at last, breathed
from innumerable throats. They were going to have their bit

of fun after all. The rifle was a beautiful German thing with cross-hair sights. I did not then know that in shooting an elephant one would shoot to cut an imaginary bar running from ear-hole to ear-hole. I ought, therefore, as the elephant was sideways on, to have aimed straight at his ear-hole; actually I aimed several inches in front of this, thinking the brain would be further forward.

When I pulled the trigger I did not hear the bang or feel the kick—one never does when a shot goes home—but I heard the devilish roar of glee that went up from the crowd. In that instant, in too short a time, one would have thought, even for the bullet to get there, a mysterious, terrible change had come over the elephant. He neither stirred nor fell, but every line of his body had altered. He looked suddenly stricken, shrunken, immensely old, as though the frightful impact of the bullet had paralysed him without knocking him down. At last, after what seemed a long time—it might have been five seconds, I dare say—he sagged flabbily to his knees. His mouth slobbered. An enormous senility seemed to have settled upon him. One could have imagined him thousands of years old. I fired again into the same spot. At the second shot he did not collapse but climbed with desperate slowness to his feet and stood weakly upright, with legs sagging and head drooping. I fired a third time. That was the shot that did for him. You could see the agony of it jolt his whole body and knock the last remnant of strength from his legs. But in falling he seemed for a moment to rise, for as his hind legs collapsed beneath him he seemed to tower upward like a huge rock toppling, his trunk reaching skywards like a tree. He trumpeted, for the first and only time. And then down he came, his belly towards me, with a crash that seemed to shake the ground even where I lay.

I got up. The Burmans were already racing past me across

the mud. It was obvious that the elephant would never rise again, but he was not dead. He was breathing very rhythmically with long rattling gasps, his great mound of a side painfully rising and falling. His mouth was wide open—I could see far down into caverns of pale pink throat. I waited a long time for him to die, but his breathing did not weaken. Finally I fired my two remaining shots into the spot where I thought his heart must be. The thick blood welled out of him like red velvet, but still he did not die. His body did not even jerk when the shots hit him, the tortured breathing continued without a pause. He was dying, very slowly and in great agony, but in some world remote from me where not even a bullet could damage him further. I felt that I had got to put an end to that dreadful noise. It seemed dreadful to see the great beast lying there, powerless to move and yet powerless to die, and not even to be able to finish him. I sent back for my small rifle and poured shot after shot into his heart and down his throat. They seemed to make no impression. The tortured gasps continued as steadily as the ticking of a clock.

In the end I could not stand it any longer and went away. I heard later that it took him half an hour to die. Burmans were bringing dahs and baskets even before I left, and I was told they had stripped his body almost to the bones by the afternoon.

Afterwards, of course, there were endless discussions about the shooting of the elephant. The owner was furious, but he was only an Indian and could do nothing. Besides, legally I had done the right thing, for a mad elephant has to be killed, like a mad dog, if its owner fails to control it. Among the Europeans opinion was divided. The older men said I was right, the younger men said it was a damn shame to shoot an elephant for killing a coolie, because an elephant was worth more than any damn Coringhee coolie. And afterwards I was very glad that the coolie had been killed; it put me legally in the right and it gave me a sufficient pretext for shooting the elephant. I often wondered whether any of the others grasped that I had done it solely to avoid looking a fool.

A Hanging

IT WAS IN BURMA, A SODDEN MORNING OF THE RAINS. A SICKLY
light, like yellow tinfoil, was slanting over the high walls into
the jail yard. We were waiting outside the condemned cells,
a row of sheds fronted with double bars, like small animal
cages. Each cell measured about ten feet by ten and was quite
bare within except for a plank bed and a pot for drinking
water. In some of them brown silent men were squatting at
the inner bars, with their blankets draped round them. These
were the condemned men, due to be hanged within the next
week or two.

One prisoner had been brought out of his cell. He was a
Hindu, a puny wisp of a man, with a shaven head and vague
liquid eyes. He had a thick, sprouting moustache, absurdly
too big for his body, rather like the moustache of a comic man
on the films. Six tall Indian warders were guarding him and
getting him ready for the gallows. Two of them stood by with
rifles and fixed bayonets, while the others handcuffed him,
passed a chain through his handcuffs and fixed it to their belts,
and lashed his arms tight to his sides. They crowded very close
about him, with their hands always on him in a careful,
caressing grip, as though all the while feeling him to make
sure he was there. It was like men handling a fish which is
still alive and may jump back into the water. But he stood
quite unresisting, yielding his arms limply to the ropes, as
though he hardly noticed what was happening.

Eight o'clock struck and a bugle call, desolately thin in the wet air, floated from the distant barracks. The superintendent of the jail, who was standing apart from the rest of us, moodily prodding the gravel with his stick, raised his head at the sound. He was an army doctor, with a grey toothbrush moustache and a gruff voice. "For God's sake hurry up, Francis," he said irritably. "The man ought to have been dead by this time. Aren't you ready yet?"

Francis, the head jailer, a fat Dravidian in a white drill suit and gold spectacles, waved his black hand. "Yes sir, yes sir," he bubbled. "All iss satisfactorily prepared. The hangman iss waiting. We shall proceed."

"Well, quick march, then. The prisoners can't get their breakfast till this job's over."

We set out for the gallows. Two warders marched on either side of the prisoner, with their rifles at the slope; two others marched close against him, gripping him by arm and shoulder, as though at once pushing and supporting him. The rest of us, magistrates and the like, followed behind. Suddenly, when we had gone ten yards, the procession stopped short without any order or warning. A dreadful thing had happened—a dog, come goodness knows whence, had appeared in the yard. It came bounding among us with a loud volley of barks, and leapt round us wagging its whole body, wild with glee at finding so many human beings together. It was a large woolly dog, half Airedale, half pariah. For a moment it pranced round us, and then, before anyone could stop it, it had made a dash for the prisoner and, jumping up, tried to lick his face. Everyone stood aghast, too taken aback even to grab at the dog.

"Who let that bloody brute in here?" said the superintendent angrily. "Catch it, someone!"

A warder, detached from the escort, charged clumsily after

the dog, but it danced and gambolled just out of his reach,
taking everything as part of the game. A young Eurasian jailer
picked up a handful of gravel and tried to stone the dog
away, but it dodged the stones and came after us again. Its
yaps echoed from the jail walls. The prisoner, in the grasp of
the two warders, looked on incuriously, as though this was
another formality of the hanging. It was several minutes before
someone managed to catch the dog. Then we put my handker-
chief through its collar and moved off once more, with the dog
still straining and whimpering.

It was about forty yards to the gallows. I watched the bare
brown back of the prisoner marching in front of me. He
walked clumsily with his bound arms, but quite steadily, with
that bobbing gait of the Indian who never straightens his
knees. At each step his muscles slid neatly into place, the lock
of hair on his scalp danced up and down, his feet printed
themselves on the wet gravel. And once, in spite of the men
who gripped him by each shoulder, he stepped slightly aside
to avoid a puddle on the path.

It is curious, but till that moment I had never realized
what it means to destroy a healthy, conscious man. When I
saw the prisoner step aside to avoid the puddle I saw the
mystery, the unspeakable wrongness, of cutting a life short
when it is in full tide. This man was not dying, he was alive
just as we are alive. All the organs of his body were working—
bowels digesting food, skin renewing itself, nails growing,
tissues forming—all toiling away in solemn foolery. His nails
would still be growing when he stood on the drop, when he
was falling through the air with a tenth-of-a-second to live.
His eyes saw the yellow gravel and the grey walls, and his
brain still remembered, foresaw, reasoned—reasoned even
about puddles. He and we were a party of men walking together, seeing, hearing, feeling, understanding the same world;

and in two minutes, with a sudden snap, one of us would be gone—one mind less, one world less.

The gallows stood in a small yard, separate from the main grounds of the prison, and overgrown with tall prickly weeds. It was a brick erection like three sides of a shed, with planking on top, and above that two beams and a crossbar with the rope dangling. The hangman, a grey-haired convict in the white uniform of the prison, was waiting beside his machine. He greeted us with a servile crouch as we entered. At a word from Francis the two warders, gripping the prisoner more closely than ever, half led half pushed him to the gallows and helped him clumsily up the ladder. Then the hangman climbed up and fixed the rope round the prisoner's neck.

We stood waiting, five yards away. The warders had formed in a rough circle round the gallows. And then, when the noose was fixed, the prisoner began crying out to his god. It was a high, reiterated cry of "Ram! Ram! Ram! Ram!" not urgent and fearful like a prayer or cry for help, but steady, rhythmical, almost like the tolling of a bell. The dog answered the sound with a whine. The hangman, still standing on the gallows, produced a small cotton bag like a flour bag and drew it down over the prisoner's face. But the sound, muffled by the cloth, still persisted, over and over again: "Ram! Ram! Ram! Ram! Ram!"

The hangman climbed down and stood ready, holding the lever. Minutes seemed to pass. The steady, muffled crying from the prisoner went on and on, "Ram! Ram! Ram!" never faltering for an instant. The superintendent, his head on his chest, was slowly poking the ground with his stick; perhaps he was counting the cries, allowing the prisoner a fixed number—fifty, perhaps, or a hundred. Everyone had changed color. The Indians had gone grey like bad coffee, and one or two of the bayonets were wavering. We looked at the lashed, hooded man on the drop, and listened to his cries—each cry another second of life; the same thought was in all our minds: oh, kill him quickly, get it over, stop that abominable noise!

Suddenly the superintendent made up his mind. Throwing up his head he made a swift motion with his stick. "Chalo!" he shouted almost fiercely.

There was a clanking noise, and then dead silence. The prisoner had vanished, and the rope was twisting on itself. I let go of the dog, and it galloped immediately to the back of the gallows; but when it got there it stopped short, barked, and then retreated into a corner of the yard, where it stood among the weeds, looking timorously out at us. We went round the gallows to inspect the prisoner's body. He was dangling with his toes pointed straight downwards, very slowly revolving, as dead as a stone.

The superintendent reached out with his stick and poked the bare brown body; it oscillated slightly. "*He's* all right," said the superintendent. He backed out from under the gallows, and blew out a deep breath. The moody look had gone out of his face quite suddenly. He glanced at his wrist-watch. "Eight minutes past eight. Well, that's all for this morning, thank God."

The warders unfixed bayonets and marched away. The dog, sobered and conscious of having misbehaved itself, slipped after them. We walked out of the gallows yard, past the condemned cells with their waiting prisoners, into the big central yard of the prison. The convicts, under the command of warders armed with lathis, were already receiving their breakfast. They squatted in long rows, each man holding a tin panikin, while two warders with buckets marched round ladling out rice; it seemed quite a homely, jolly scene, after the hanging. An enormous relief had come upon us now that the job was done. One felt an impulse to sing, to break into a run, to snigger. All at once everyone began chattering gaily.

The Eurasian boy walking beside me nodded towards the

way we had come, with a knowing smile: "Do you know, sir, our friend [he meant the dead man] when he heard his appeal had been dismissed, he pissed on the floor of his cell. From fright. Kindly take one of my cigarettes, sir. Do you not admire my new silver case, sir? From the boxwalah, two rupees eight annas. Classy European style."

Several people laughed—at what, nobody seemed certain.

Francis was walking by the superintendent, talking garrulously: "Well, sir, all hass passed off with the utmost satisfactoriness. It was all finished—flick! like that. It iss not always so—oah, no! I have known cases where the doctor wass obliged to go beneath the gallows and pull the prissoner's legs to ensure decease. Most disagreeable!"

"Wriggling about, eh? That's bad," said the superintendent.

"Ach, sir, it iss worse when they become refractory! One man, I recall, clung to the bars of hiss cage when we went to take him out. You will scarcely credit, sir, that it took six warders to dislodge him, three pulling at each leg. We reasoned with him. 'My dear fellow,' we said, 'think of all the pain and trouble you are causing to us!' But no, he would not listen! Ach, he wass very troublesome!"

I found that I was laughing quite loudly. Everyone was laughing. Even the superintendent grinned in a tolerant way. "You'd better all come out and have a drink," he said quite genially. "I've got a bottle of whisky in the car. We could do with it."

We went through the big double gates of the prison into the road. "Pulling at his legs!" exclaimed a Burmese magistrate suddenly, and burst into a loud chuckling. We all began laughing again. At that moment Francis' anecdote seemed extraordinarily funny. We all had a drink together, native and European alike, quite amicably. The dead man was a hundred yards away.

How the Poor Die

IN THE YEAR 1929 I SPENT SEVERAL WEEKS IN THE HÔPITAL X, IN the fifteenth arrondissement of Paris. The clerks put me through the usual third-degree at the reception desk, and indeed I was kept answering questions for some twenty minutes before they would let me in. If you have ever had to fill up forms in a Latin country you will know the kind of questions I mean. For some days past I had been unequal to translating Reaumur into Fahrenheit, but I know that my temperature was round about 103, and by the end of the interview I had some difficulty in standing on my feet. At my back a resigned little knot of patients, carrying bundles done up in colored handkerchiefs, waited their turn to be questioned.

After the questioning came the bath—a compulsory routine for all newcomers, apparently, just as in prison or the workhouse. My clothes were taken away from me, and after I had sat shivering for some minutes in five inches of warm water I was given a linen nightshirt and a short blue flannel dressing-gown—no slippers, they had none big enough for me, they said—and led out into the open air. This was a night in February and I was suffering from pneumonia. The ward we were going to was 200 yards away and it seemed that to get to it you had to cross the hospital grounds. Someone stumbled in front of me with a lantern. The gravel path was frosty underfoot, and the wind whipped the nightshirt round my bare calves. When we got into the ward I was aware of a strange feeling of familiarity whose origin I did not succeed in pinning down till later in the night. It was a long, rather low, ill-lit room, full of murmuring voices and with three rows of beds surprisingly close together. There was a foul smell, faecal and yet sweetish. As I lay down I saw on a bed nearly opposite me a small, round-shouldered, sandy-haired man sitting half naked while a doctor and a student performed some strange operation on him. First the doctor produced from his black bag a dozen small glasses like wine glasses, then the student burned a match inside each glass to exhaust the air, then the glass was popped on to the man's back or chest and the vacuum drew up a huge yellow blister. Only after some moments did I realize what they were doing to him. It was something called cupping, a treatment which you can read about in old medical textbooks but which till then I had vaguely thought of as one of those things they do to horses.

The cold air outside had probably lowered my temperature, and I watched this barbarous remedy with detachment and even a certain amount of amusement. The next moment, however, the doctor and the student came across to my bed, hoisted me upright and without a word began applying the same set of glasses, which had not been sterilized in any way. A few feeble protests that I uttered got no more response than if I had been an animal. I was very much impressed by the impersonal way in which the two men started on me. I had never been in the public ward of a hospital before, and it was my first experience of doctors who handle you without speaking to you or, in a human sense, taking any notice of you. They only put on six glasses in my case, but after doing so they scarified the blisters and applied the glasses again. Each glass now drew out about a dessert-spoonful of dark-colored blood. As I lay down again, humiliated, disgusted and frightened by the thing that had been done to me, I reflected that now at least they would leave me alone. But no, not a bit of it. There was another treatment coming, the mustard poultice, seemingly a matter of routine like the hot bath. Two slatternly nurses had already got the poultice ready, and they lashed it round my chest as tight as a strait-jacket while some men who were wandering about the ward in shirt and trousers began to collect round my bed with half-sympathetic grins. I learned later that watching a patient have a mustard poultice was a favorite pastime in the ward. These things are normally applied for a quarter of an hour and certainly they are funny enough if you don't happen to be the person inside. For the first five minutes the pain is severe, but you believe you can bear it. During the second five minutes this belief evaporates, but the poultice is buckled at the back and you can't get it off. This is the period the onlookers enjoy most. During the last five minutes, I noted, a sort of numbness supervenes. After the poultice had been removed a waterproof pillow packed with ice was thrust beneath my head and I was left alone. I did not sleep, and to the best of my knowledge this was the only night of my life—I mean the only night spent in bed—in which I have not slept at all, not even a minute.

During my first hour in the Hôpital X I had had a whole series of different and contradictory treatments, but this was misleading, for in general you got very little treatment at all, either good or bad, unless you were ill in some interesting and instructive way. At five in the morning the nurses came round, woke the patients and took their temperatures, but did not wash them. If you were well enough you washed yourself, otherwise you depended on the kindness of some walking patient. It was generally patients, too, who carried the bed-bottles and the grim bedpan, nicknamed *la casserole*. At eight breakfast arrived, called army-fashion *la soupe*. It was soup, too, a thin vegetable soup with slimy hunks of bread floating about in it. Later in the day the tall, solemn, black-bearded doctor made his rounds, with an interne and a troop of students following at his heels, but there were about sixty of us in the ward and it was evident that he had other wards to attend to as well. There were many beds past which he walked day after day, sometimes followed by imploring cries. On the other hand if you had some disease with which the students wanted to familiarize themselves you got plenty of attention of a kind. I myself, with an exceptionally fine specimen of a bronchial rattle, sometimes had as many as a dozen students queuing up to listen to my chest. It was a very queer feeling— queer, I mean, because of their intense interest in learning their job, together with a seeming lack of any perception that the patients were human beings. It is strange to relate, but sometimes as some young student stepped forward to take his turn at manipulating you, he would be actually tremulous with excitement, like a boy who has at last got his hands on some expensive piece of machinery. And then ear after ear—ears of young men, of girls, of Negroes—pressed against your back, relays of fingers solemnly but clumsily tapping, and not from any one of them did you get a word of conversation or a look direct in your face. As a non-paying patient, in the uniform nightshirt, you were primarily *a specimen*, a thing I did not resent but could never quite get used to.

After some days I grew well enough to sit up and study the surrounding patients. The stuffy room, with its narrow beds so close together that you could easily touch your neighbor's hand, had every sort of disease in it except, I suppose, acutely infectious cases. My right-hand neighbor was a little red-haired cobbler with one leg shorter than the other, who used to announce the death of any other patient (this happened a number of times, and my neighbor was always the first to hear of it) by whistling to me, exclaiming "Numero 43!" (or whatever it was) and flinging his arms above his head. This man had not much wrong with him, but in most of the other beds within my angle of vision some squalid tragedy or some plain horror was being enacted. In the bed that was foot to foot with mine there lay, until he died (I didn't see him die—they moved him to another bed), a little weazened man who was suffering from I do not know what disease, but something that made his whole body so intensely sensitive that any movement from side to side, sometimes even the weight of the bedclothes, would make him shout out with pain. His worst suffering was when he urinated, which he did with the greatest difficulty. A nurse would bring him the bedbottle and then for a long time stand beside his bed, whistling, as grooms are said to do with horses, until at last with an agonized shriek of *"Je pisse!"* he would get started. In the bed next to him the sandy-haired man whom I had seen being cupped used to cough up blood-streaked mucus at all hours. My left-hand neighbor was a tall, flaccid-looking young man who used periodically to have a tube inserted into his back and astonishing quantities of frothy liquid drawn off from some part of his body. In the bed beyond that a veteran of the war of 1870 was dying, a handsome old man with a white imperial, round whose bed, at all hours when visiting was allowed, four elderly female relatives dressed all in black sat exactly like crows, obviously scheming for some pitiful legacy. In the bed opposite me in the further row was an old baldheaded man with drooping moustaches and greatly swollen face and body, who was suffering from some disease that made him urinate almost incessantly. A huge glass receptacle stood always beside his bed. One day his wife and daughter came to visit him. At sight of them the old man's bloated face lit up with a smile of surprising sweetness, and as his daughter, a pretty girl of about twenty, approached the bed

I saw that his hand was slowly working its way from under the
bedclothes. I seemed to see in advance the gesture that was
coming—the girl kneeling beside the bed, the old man's hand
laid on her head in his dying blessing. But no, he merely
handed her the bedbottle, which she promptly took from him
and emptied into the receptacle.

About a dozen beds away from me was Numero 57—I think
that was his number—a cirrhosis of the liver case. Everyone in
the ward knew him by sight because he was sometimes the
subject of a medical lecture. On two afternoons a week the
tall, grave doctor would lecture in the ward to a party of students, and on more than one occasion old Numero 57 was
wheeled in on a sort of trolley into the middle of the ward,
where the doctor would roll back his nightshirt, dilate with
his fingers a huge flabby protuberance on the man's belly—
the diseased liver, I suppose—and explain solemnly that this
was a disease attributable to alcoholism, commoner in the
wine-drinking countries. As usual he neither spoke to his
patient nor gave him a smile, a nod or any kind of recognition.
While he talked, very grave and upright, he would hold the
wasted body beneath his two hands, sometimes giving it a
gentle roll to and fro, in just the attitude of a woman handling
a rolling-pin. Not that Numero 57 minded this kind of thing.
Obviously he was an old hospital inmate, a regular exhibit at
lectures, his liver long since marked down for a bottle in
some pathological museum. Utterly uninterested in what was
said about him, he would lie with his colorless eyes gazing at
nothing, while the doctor showed him off like a piece of an-
tique china. He was a man of about sixty, astonishingly
shrunken. His face, pale as vellum, had shrunken away till it
seemed no bigger than a doll's.

One morning my cobbler neighbor woke me up plucking at
my pillow before the nurses arrived. "Numero 57!"—he flung

his arms above his head. There was a light in the ward, enough to see by. I could see old Numero 57 lying crumpled up on his side, his face sticking out over the side of the bed, and towards me. He had died some time during the night, nobody knew when. When the nurses came they received the news of his death indifferently and went about their work. After a long time, an hour or more, two other nurses marched in abreast like soldiers, with a great clumping of sabots, and knotted the corpse up in the sheets, but it was not removed till some time later. Meanwhile, in the better light, I had had time for a good look at Numero 57. Indeed I lay on my side to look at him. Curiously enough he was the first dead European I had seen. I had seen dead men before, but always Asiatics and usually people who had died violent deaths. Numero 57's eyes were still open, his mouth also open, his small face contorted into an expression of agony. What most impressed me, however, was the whiteness of his face. It had been pale before, but now it was little darker than the sheets. As I gazed at the tiny, screwed-up face it struck me that this disgusting piece of refuse, waiting to be carted away and dumped on a slab in the dissecting room, was an example of "natural" death, one of the things you pray for in the Litany. There you are, then, I thought, that's what is waiting for you, twenty, thirty, forty years hence: that is how the lucky ones die, the one who lives to be old. One wants to live, of course, indeed one only stays alive by virtue of the fear of death, but I think now, as I thought then, that it's better to die violently and not too old. People talk about the horrors of war, but what weapon has man invented that even approaches in cruelty some of the commoner diseases? "Natural" death, almost by definition, means something slow, smelly and painful. Even at that, it makes a difference if you can achieve it in your own home and not in a public institution. This poor old wretch who had just flickered out like a candle-end was not even important enough to have anyone watching by his deathbed. He was merely a number, then a "subject" for the students' scalpels. And the sordid publicity of dying in such a place! In the Hôpital X the beds were very close together and there were no screens. Fancy, for instance, dying like the little man whose bed was for a while foot to foot with mine, the one who cried out when the bedclothes touched him! I dare say *"Je pisse!"* were his last recorded words. Perhaps the dying don't bother about such things—that at least would be the standard answer: nevertheless dying people are often more or less normal in their minds till within a day or so of the end.

In the public wards of a hospital you see horrors that you don't seem to meet with among people who manage to die in their own homes, as though certain diseases only attacked people at the lower income levels. But it is a fact that you would not in any English hospitals see some of the things I saw in the Hôpital X. This business of people just dying like animals, for instance, with nobody standing by, nobody interested, the death not even noticed till the morning—this happened more than once. You certainly would not see that in England, and still less would you see a corpse left exposed to the view of the other patients. I remember that once in a cottage hospital in England a man died while we were at tea, and though there were only six of us in the ward the nurses managed things so adroitly that the man was dead and his body removed without our even hearing about it till tea was over. A thing we perhaps underrate in England is the advantage we enjoy in having large numbers of well-trained and rigidly-disciplined nurses. No doubt English nurses are dumb enough, they may tell fortunes with tea-leaves, wear Union Jack badges and keep photographs of the Queen on their mantelpieces, but at least they don't let you lie unwashed

and constipated on an unmade bed, out of sheer laziness. The
nurses at the Hôpital X still had a tinge of Mrs. Gamp about
them, and later, in the military hospitals of Republican Spain,
I was to see nurses almost too ignorant to take a temperature.
You wouldn't, either, see in England such dirt as existed in
the Hôpital X. Later on, when I was well enough to wash
myself in the bathroom, I found that there was kept there a
huge packing case into which the scraps of food and dirty
dressings from the ward were flung, and the wainscotings
were infested by crickets.

When I had got back my clothes and grown strong on my
legs I fled from the Hôpital X, before my time was up and
without waiting for a medical discharge. It was not the only
hospital I have fled from, but its gloom and bareness, its sickly
smell and, above all, something in its mental atmosphere stand
out in my memory as exceptional. I had been taken there because it was the hospital belonging to my arrondissement, and
I did not learn till after I was in it that it bore a bad reputation. A year or two later the celebrated swindler, Madame
Hanaud, who was ill while on remand, was taken to the
Hôpital X, and after a few days of it she managed to elude
her guards, took a taxi and drove back to the prison, explain-
ing that she was more comfortable there. I have no doubt
that the Hôpital X was quite untypical of French hospitals
even at that date. But the patients, nearly all of them working
men, were surprisingly resigned. Some of them seemed to find
the conditions almost comfortable, for at least two were destitute malingerers who found this a good way of getting through
the winter. The nurses connived because the malingerers made
themselves useful by doing odd jobs. But the attitude of the
majority was: of course this is a lousy place, but what else do
you expect? It did not seem strange to them that you should
be woken at five and then wait three hours before starting the

day on watery soup, or that people should die with no one at
their bedside, or even that your chance of getting medical
attention should depend on catching the doctor's eye as he
went past. According to their traditions that was what hospitals were like. If you are seriously ill, and if you are too
poor to be treated in your own home, then you must go into
hospital, and once there you must put up with harshness and
discomfort, just as you would in the army. But on top of this
I was interested to find a lingering belief in the old stories
that have now almost faded from memory in England—stories,
for instance, about doctors cutting you open out of sheer
curiosity or thinking it funny to start operating before you
were properly "under." There were dark tales about a little
operating-room said to be situated just beyond the bathroom.
Dreadful screams were said to issue from this room. I saw
nothing to confirm these stories and no doubt they were all
nonsense, though I did see two students kill a sixteen-year-old
boy, or nearly kill him (he appeared to be dying when I left
the hospital, but he may have recovered later) by a mischie-
vous experiment which they probably could not have tried on
a paying patient. Well within living memory it used to be
believed in London that in some of the big hospitals patients
were killed off to get dissection subjects. I didn't hear this tale
repeated at the Hôpital X, but I should think some of the
men there would have found it credible. For it was a hospital
in which not the methods, perhaps, but something of the atmosphere of the nineteenth century had managed to survive,
and therein lay its peculiar interest.

During the past fifty years or so there has been a great
change in the relationship between doctor and patient. If you
look at almost any literature before the later part of the
nineteenth century, you find that a hospital is popularly regarded as much the same thing as a prison, and an old-

fashioned, dungeon-like prison at that. A hospital is a place
of filth, torture and death, a sort of antechamber to the tomb.
No one who was not more or less destitute would have thought
of going into such a place for treatment. And especially in
the early part of the last century, when medical science had
grown bolder than before without being any more successful,
the whole business of doctoring was looked on with horror
and dread by ordinary people. Surgery, in particular, was believed to be no more than a peculiarly gruesome form of
sadism, and dissection, possible only with the aid of body-
snatchers, was even confused with necromancy. From the nineteenth century you could collect a large horror-literature connected with doctors and hospitals. Think of poor old George
III, in his dotage, shrieking for mercy as he sees his surgeons
approaching to "bleed him till he faints"! Think of the conversations of Bob Sawyer and Benjamin Allen, which no doubt
are hardly parodies, or the field hospitals in *La Débacle* and
War and Peace, or that shocking description of an amputa-
tion in Melville's *Whitejacket!* Even the names given to doctors in nineteenth-century English fiction, Slasher, Carver,
Sawyer, Fillgrave and so on, and the generic nickname "saw-
bones," are about as grim as they are comic. The anti-surgery
tradition is perhaps best expressed in Tennyson's poem, *The
Children's Hospital,* which is essentially a pre-chloroform
document though it seems to have been written as late as
1880. Moreover, the outlook which Tennyson records in this
poem had a lot to be said for it. When you consider what an
operation without anaesthetics must have been like, what it
notoriously *was* like, it is difficult not to suspect the motives
of people who would undertake such things. For these bloody
horrors which the students so eagerly looked forward to
("A magnificent sight if Slasher does it!") were admittedly
more or less useless: the patient who did not die of shock

usually died of gangrene, a result which was taken for granted.
Even now doctors can be found whose motives are question-
able. Anyone who has had much illness, or who has listened
to medical students talking, will know what I mean. But
anaesthetics were a turning point, and disinfectants were
another. Nowhere in the world, probably, would you now see
the kind of scene described by Axel Munthe in *The Story of
San Michele*, when the sinister surgeon in top hat and frock
coat, his starched shirtfront spattered with blood and pus,
carves up patient after patient with the same knife and flings
the severed limbs into a pile beside the table. Moreover, national health insurance has partly done away with the idea
that a working-class patient is a pauper who deserves little
consideration. Well into this century it was usual for "free"
patients at the big hospitals to have their teeth extracted with
no anaesthetic. They didn't pay, so why should they have an
anaesthetic—that was the attitude. That too has changed.

And yet every institution will always bear upon it some lingering memory of its past. A barrack-room is still haunted by
the ghost of Kipling, and it is difficult to enter a workhouse
without being reminded of *Oliver Twist*. Hospitals began as
a kind of casual ward for lepers and the like to die in, and
they continued as places where medical students learned their
art on the bodies of the poor. You can still catch a faint suggestion of their history in their characteristically gloomy architecture. I would be far from complaining about the treatment
I have received in any English hospital, but I do know that it
is a sound instinct that warns people to keep out of hospitals
if possible, and especially out of the public wards. Whatever
the legal position may be, it is unquestionable that you have
far less control over your own treatment, far less certainty that
frivolous experiments will not be tried on you, when it is a
case of "accept the discipline or get out." And it is a great

thing to die in your own bed, though it is better still to die in your boots. However great the kindness and the efficiency, in every hospital death there will be some cruel, squalid detail, something perhaps too small to be told but leaving terribly painful memories behind, arising out of the haste, the crowding, the impersonality of a place where every day people are dying among strangers.

The dread of hospitals probably still survives among the very poor, and in all of us it has only recently disappeared. It is a dark patch not far beneath the surface of our minds. I have said earlier that when I entered the ward at the Hôpital X I was conscious of a strange feeling of familiarity. What the scene reminded me of, of course, was the reeking, pain-filled hospitals of the nineteenth century, which I had never seen but of which I had a traditional knowledge. And something, perhaps the black-clad doctor with his frowsy black bag, or perhaps only the sickly smell, played the queer trick of unearthing from my memory that poem of Tennyson's, *The Children's Hospital,* which I had not thought of for twenty years. It happened that as a child I had had it read aloud to me by a sick-nurse whose own working life might have stretched back to the time when Tennyson wrote the poem. The horrors and sufferings of the old-style hospitals were a vivid memory to her. We had shuddered over the poem together, and then seemingly I had forgotten it. Even its name would probably have recalled nothing to me. But the first glimpse of the ill-lit murmurous room, with the beds so close together, suddenly roused the train of thought to which it belonged, and in the night that followed I found myself remembering the whole story and atmosphere of the poem, with many of its lines complete.

Lear, Tolstoy and the Fool

TOLSTOY'S PAMPHLETS ARE THE LEAST-KNOWN PART OF HIS WORK, and his attack on Shakespeare [1] is not even an easy document to get hold of, at any rate in an English translation. Perhaps, therefore, it will be useful if I give a summary of the pamphlet before trying to discuss it.

Tolstoy begins by saying that throughout life Shakespeare has aroused in him "an irresistible repulsion and tedium." Conscious that the opinion of the civilized world is against him, he has made one attempt after another on Shakespeare's works, reading and re-reading them in Russian, English and German; but "I invariably underwent the same feelings; repulsion, weariness and bewilderment." Now, at the age of seventy-five, he has once again re-read the entire works of Shakespeare, including the historical plays, and

I have felt with an even greater force, the same feelings—this time, however, not of bewilderment, but of firm, indubitable conviction that the unquestionable glory of a great genius which Shakespeare enjoys, and which compels writers of our time to imitate him and readers and spectators to discover in him non-existent merits—thereby distorting their aesthetic and ethical understanding—is a great evil, as is every untruth.

Shakespeare, Tolstoy adds, is not merely no genius, but is not even "an average author," and in order to demonstrate

[1] *Shakespeare and the Drama.* Written about 1903 as an introduction to another pamphlet, *Shakespeare and the Working Classes,* by Ernest Crosby.

this fact he will examine *King Lear,* which, as he is able to show by quotations from Hazlitt, Brandes and others, has been extravagantly praised and can be taken as an example of Shakespeare's best work.

Tolstoy then makes a sort of exposition of the plot of *King Lear,* finding it at every step to be stupid, verbose, unnatural, unintelligible, bombastic, vulgar, tedious and full of incredible events, "wild ravings," "mirthless jokes," anachronisms, irrelevancies, obscenities, worn-out stage conventions and other faults both moral and aesthetic. *Lear* is, in any case, a plagiarism of an earlier and much better play, *King Leir,* by an unknown author, which Shakespeare stole and then ruined. It is worth quoting a specimen paragraph to illustrate the manner in which Tolstoy goes to work. Act III, Scene 2 (in which Lear, Kent and the Fool are together in the storm) is summarized thus:

Lear walks about the heath and says words which are meant to express his despair: he desires that the winds should blow so hard that they (the winds) should crack their cheeks and that the rain should flood everything, that lightning should singe his white head, and the thunder flatten the world and destroy all germs "that make ungrateful man"! The fool keeps uttering still more senseless words. Enter Kent: Lear says that for some reason during this storm all criminals shall be found out and convicted. Kent, still unrecognized by Lear, endeavors to persuade him to take refuge in a hovel. At this point the fool utters a prophecy in no wise related to the situation and they all depart.

Tolstoy's final verdict on *Lear* is that no unhypnotized observer, if such an observer existed, could read it to the end with any feeling except "aversion and weariness." And exactly the same is true of "all the other extolled dramas of Shakespeare, not to mention the senseless dramatized tales, *Pericles, Twelfth Night, The Tempest, Cymbeline, Troilus and Cressida.*"

Having dealt with *Lear* Tolstoy draws up a more general indictment against Shakespeare. He finds that Shakespeare has a certain technical skill which is partly traceable to his having been an actor, but otherwise no merits whatever. He has no power of delineating character or of making words and actions spring naturally out of situations, his language is uniformly exaggerated and ridiculous, he constantly thrusts his own random thoughts into the mouth of any character who happens to be handy, he displays a "complete absence of aesthetic feeling," and his words "have nothing whatever in common with art and poetry."

"Shakespeare might have been whatever you like," Tolstoy concludes, "but he was not an artist." Moreover, his opinions are not original or interesting, and his tendency is "of the lowest and most immoral." Curiously enough, Tolstoy does not base this last judgment on Shakespeare's own utterances, but on the statements of two critics, Gervinus and Brandes. According to Gervinus (or at any rate Tolstoy's reading of Gervinus) "Shakespeare taught . . . that one *may be too good*," while according to Brandes: "Shakespeare's fundamental principle . . . is that *the end justifies the means.*" Tolstoy adds on his own account that Shakespeare was a jingo patriot of the worst type, but apart from this he considers that Gervinus and Brandes have given a true and adequate description of Shakespeare's view of life.

Tolstoy then recapitulates in a few paragraphs the theory of art which he had expressed at greater length elsewhere. Put still more shortly, it amounts to a demand for dignity of subject matter, sincerity, and good craftsmanship. A great work of art must deal with some subject which is "important to the life of mankind," it must express something which the author genuinely feels, and it must use such technical methods as will produce the desired effect. As Shakespeare is debased in outlook, slipshod in execution and incapable of being sincere even for a moment, he obviously stands condemned.

But here there arises a difficult question. If Shakespeare is all that Tolstoy has shown him to be, how did he ever come to be so generally admired? Evidently the answer can only lie in a sort of mass hypnosis, or "epidemic suggestion." The whole civilized world has somehow been deluded into thinking Shakespeare a good writer, and even the plainest demonstration to the contrary makes no impression, because one is not dealing with a reasoned opinion but with something akin to religious faith. Throughout history, says Tolstoy, there has been an endless series of these "epidemic suggestions"—for example, the Crusades, the search for the Philosopher's Stone, the craze for tulip growing which once swept over Holland, and so on and so forth. As a contemporary instance he cites, rather significantly, the Dreyfus case over which the whole world grew violently excited for no sufficient reason. There are also sudden short-lived crazes for new political and philosophical theories, or for this or that writer, artist or scientist—for example, Darwin who (in 1903) is "beginning to be forgotten." And in some cases a quite worthless popular idol may remain in favor for centuries, for "it also happens that such crazes, having arisen in consequence of special reasons accidentally favoring their establishment, correspond in such a degree to the views of life spread in society, and especially in literary circles, that they are maintained for a long time." Shakespeare's plays have continued to be admired over a long period because "they corresponded to the irreligious and immoral frame of mind of the upper classes of his time and ours."

As to the manner in which Shakespeare's fame *started,* Tolstoy explains it as having been "got up" by German professors towards the end of the eighteenth century. His reputation "originated in Germany, and thence was transferred to England." The Germans chose to elevate Shakespeare because, at a time when there was no German drama worth speaking about and French classical literature was beginning to seem frigid and artificial, they were captivated by Shakespeare's "clever development of scenes" and also found in him a good expression of their own attitude towards life. Goethe pronounced Shakespeare a great poet, whereupon all the other critics flocked after him like a troop of parrots, and the general infatuation has lasted ever since. The result has been a further debasement of the drama—Tolstoy is careful to include his own plays when condemning the contemporary stage—and a further corruption of the prevailing moral outlook. It follows that "the false glorification of Shakespeare" is an important evil which Tolstoy feels it his duty to combat.

This, then, is the substance of Tolstoy's pamphlet. One's first feeling is that in describing Shakespeare as a bad writer he is saying something demonstrably untrue. But this is not the case. In reality there is no kind of evidence or argument by which one can show that Shakespeare, or any other writer, is "good." Nor is there any way of definitely proving that— for instance—Warwick Deeping is "bad." Ultimately there is no test of literary merit except survival, which is itself an index to majority opinion. Artistic theories such as Tolstoy's are quite worthless, because they not only start out with arbitrary assumptions, but depend on vague terms ("sincere," "important," and so forth) which can be interpreted in any way one chooses. Properly speaking one cannot *answer* Tolstoy's attack. The interesting question is: why did he make it? But it should be noticed in passing that he uses many weak or dishonest arguments. Some of these are worth pointing out, not because they invalidate his main charge but because they are, so to speak, evidence of malice.

To begin with, his examination of *King Lear* is not "impartial," as he twice claims. On the contrary, it is a prolonged exercise in misrepresentation. It is obvious that when you are summarizing *King Lear* for the benefit of someone who has not read it, you are not really being impartial if you introduce an important speech (Lear's speech when Cordelia is dead in his arms) in this manner: "Again begin Lear's awful ravings, at which one feels ashamed, as at unsuccessful jokes." And in a long series of instances Tolstoy slightly alters or colors the passages he is criticizing, always in such a way as to make the plot appear a little more complicated and improbable, or the language a little more exaggerated. For example, we are told that Lear "has no necessity or motive for his abdication," although his reason for abdicating (that he is old and wishes to retire from the cares of state) has been clearly indicated in the first scene. It will be seen that even in the passage which I quoted earlier, Tolstoy has wilfully misunderstood one phrase and slightly changed the meaning of another, making nonsense of a remark which is reasonable enough in its context. None of these mis-readings is very gross in itself, but their cumulative effect is to exaggerate the psychological incoherence of the play. Again, Tolstoy is not able to explain why Shakespeare's plays were still in print, and still on the stage, two hundred years after his death (*before* the "epidemic suggestion" started, that is); and his whole account of Shakespeare's rise to fame is guesswork punctuated by outright misstatements. And again, various of his accusations contradict one another: for example, Shakespeare is a mere entertainer and "not in earnest," but on the other hand he is constantly putting his own thoughts into the mouths of his characters. On the whole it is difficult to feel that Tolstoy's criticisms are uttered in good faith. In any case it is impossible that he should fully have believed in his main thesis—believed, that is to say, that for a century or more the entire civilized world had been taken in by a huge and palpable lie which he alone was able to see through. Certainly his dislike of Shakespeare is real enough, but the reasons for it may be different, or partly different, from what he avows; and therein lies the interest of his pamphlet.

At this point one is obliged to start guessing. However, there is one possible clue, or at least there is a question which may point the way to a clue. It is: why did Tolstoy, with thirty or more plays to choose from, pick out *King Lear* as his especial target? True *Lear* is so well-known and has been so much praised that it could justly be taken as representative of Shakespeare's best work; still, for the purpose of a hostile analysis Tolstoy would probably choose the play he disliked most. Is it not possible that he bore an especial enmity towards this particular play because he was aware, consciously or unconsciously, of the resemblance between Lear's story and his own? But it is better to approach this clue from the opposite direction—that is, by examining *Lear* itself, and the qualities in it that Tolstoy fails to mention.

One of the first things an English reader would notice in Tolstoy's pamphlet is that it hardly deals with Shakespeare as a poet. Shakespeare is treated as a dramatist, and in so far as his popularity is not spurious, it is held to be due to tricks of stagecraft which give good opportunities to clever actors. Now, so far as the English-speaking countries go, this is not true. Several of the plays which are most valued by lovers of Shakespeare (for instance, *Timon of Athens*) are seldom or never acted, while some of the most actable such as *A Midsummer Night's Dream,* are the least admired. Those who care most for Shakespeare value him in the first place for his use of language, the "verbal music" which even Bernard Shaw, another hostile critic, admits to be "irresistible." Tolstoy ignores this, and does not seem to realize that a poem may have a special value for those who speak the language in which it was written. However, even if one puts oneself in Tolstoy's place and tries to think of Shakespeare as a foreign poet it is still clear that there is something that Tolstoy has left out. Poetry, it seems, is *not* solely a matter of sound and association, and valueless outside its own language-group: otherwise how is it that some poems, including poems written in dead languages, succeed in crossing frontiers? Clearly a lyric like "Tomorrow is Saint Valentine's Day" could not be satisfactorily translated, but in Shakespeare's major work there is something describable as poetry that can be separated from the words. Tolstoy is right in saying that *Lear* is not a very good play, as a play. It is too drawn-out and has too many characters and sub-plots. One wicked daughter would have been quite enough, and Edgar is a superfluous character: indeed it would probably be a better play if Gloucester and both his sons were eliminated. Nevertheless, something, a kind of pattern, or perhaps only an atmosphere, survives the complications and the *longueurs*. *Lear* can be imagined as a puppet show, a mime, a ballet, a series of pictures. Part of its poetry, perhaps the most essential part, is inherent in the story and is dependent neither on any particular set of words, nor on flesh-and-blood presentation.

Shut your eyes and think of *King Lear*, if possible without calling to mind any of the dialogue. What do you see? Here at any rate is what I see: a majestic old man in a long black robe, with flowing white hair and beard, a figure out of Blake's drawings (but also, curiously enough, rather like Tolstoy), wandering through a storm and cursing the heavens, in company with a Fool and a lunatic. Presently the scene shifts and the old man, still cursing, still understanding nothing, is hold-

ing a dead girl in his arms while the Fool dangles on a gallows somewhere in the background. This is the bare skeleton
of the play, and even here Tolstoy wants to cut out most of
what is essential. He objects to the storm, as being unnecessary, to the Fool, who in his eyes is simply a tedious nuisance
and an excuse for making bad jokes, and to the death of Cordelia, which, as he sees it, robs the play of its moral. According
to Tolstoy, the earlier play, *King Leir,* which Shakespeare
adapted

terminates more naturally and more in accordance with the moral
demands of the spectator than does Shakespeare's: namely, by the
King of the Gauls conquering the husbands of the elder sisters, and
by Cordelia, instead of being killed, restoring Leir to his former
position.

In other words the tragedy ought to have been a comedy, or
perhaps a melodrama. It is doubtful whether the sense of
tragedy is compatible with belief in God: at any rate, it is
not compatible with disbelief in human dignity and with the
kind of "moral demand" which feels cheated when virtue fails
to triumph. A tragic situation exists precisely when virtue
does *not* triumph but when it is still felt that man is nobler
than the forces which destroy him. It is perhaps more significant that Tolstoy sees no justification for the presence of the
Fool. The Fool is integral to the play. He acts not only as a
sort of chorus, making the central situation clearer by commenting on it more intelligently than the other characters, but
as a foil to Lear's frenzies. His jokes, riddles and scraps of
rhyme, and his endless digs at Lear's high-minded folly, rang-
ing from mere derision to a sort of melancholy poetry ("All
thy other titles thou hast given away; that thou wast born
with"), are like a trickle of sanity running through the play,
a reminder that somewhere or other in spite of the injustices,

cruelties, intrigues, deceptions and misunderstandings that are being enacted here, life is going on much as usual. In Tolstoy's impatience with the Fool one gets a glimpse of his deeper quarrel with Shakespeare. He objects, with some justification, to the raggedness of Shakespeare's plays, the irrelevancies, the incredible plots, the exaggerated language: but what at bottom he probably most dislikes is a sort of exuberance, a tendency to take—not so much a pleasure as simply an interest in the actual process of life. It is a mistake to write Tolstoy off as a moralist attacking an artist. He never said that art, as such, is wicked or meaningless, nor did he even say that technical virtuosity is unimportant. But his main aim, in his later years, was to narrow the range of human consciousness. One's interests, one's points of attachment to the physical world and the day-to-day struggle, must be as few and not as many as possible. Literature must consist of parables, stripped of detail and almost independent of language. The parables—this is where Tolstoy differs from the average vulgar puritan—must themselves be works of art, but pleasure and curiosity must be excluded from them. Science, also, must be divorced from curiosity. The business of science, he says, is not to discover what happens but to teach men how they ought to live. So also with history and politics. Many problems (for example, the Dreyfus case) are simply not worth solving, and he is willing to leave them as loose ends. Indeed his whole theory of "crazes" or "epidemic suggestions," in which he lumps together such things as the Crusades and the Dutch passion of tulip growing, shows a willingness to regard many human activities as mere ant-like rushings to and fro, inexplicable and uninteresting. Clearly he could have no patience with a chaotic, detailed, discursive writer like Shakespeare. His reaction is that of an irritable old man who is being pestered by a noisy child. "Why do you keep jumping up and down like

that? Why can't you sit still like I do?" In a way the old man
is in the right, but the trouble is that the child has a feeling
in its limbs which the old man has lost. And if the old man
knows of the existence of this feeling, the effect is merely to
increase his irritation: he would make children senile, if he
could. Tolstoy does not know, perhaps, just *what* he misses
in Shakespeare, but he is aware that he misses something, and
he is determined that others shall be deprived of it as well. By
nature he was imperious as well as egotistical. Well after he
was grown up he would still occasionally strike his servant in
moments of anger, and somewhat later, according to his English biographer, Derrick Leon, he felt "a frequent desire upon
the slenderest provocation to slap the faces of those with
whom he disagreed." One does not necessarily get rid of that
kind of temperament by undergoing religious conversion, and
indeed it is obvious that the illusion of having been reborn
may allow one's native vices to flourish more freely than ever,
though perhaps in subtler forms. Tolstoy was capable of ab-
juring physical violence and of seeing what this implies, but
he was not capable of tolerance or humility, and even if one
knew nothing of his other writings, one could deduce his
tendency towards spiritual bullying from this single pamphlet.

However, Tolstoy is not simply trying to rob others of a
pleasure he does not share. He is doing that, but his quarrel
with Shakespeare goes further. It is the quarrel between the
religious and the humanist attitudes towards life. Here one
comes back to the central theme of *King Lear*, which Tolstoy
does not mention, although he sets forth the plot in some
detail.

Lear is one of the minority of Shakespeare's plays that are
unmistakably *about* something. As Tolstoy justly complains,
much rubbish has been written about Shakespeare as a philosopher, as a psychologist, as a "great moral teacher," and

what-not. Shakespeare was not a systematic thinker, his most serious thoughts are uttered irrelevantly or indirectly, and we do not know to what extent he wrote with a "purpose" or even how much of the work attributed him was actually written by him. In the sonnets he never even refers to the plays as part of his achievement, though he does make what seems to be a half-ashamed allusion to his career as an actor. It is perfectly possible that he looked on at least half of his plays as mere pot-boilers and hardly bothered about purpose or probability so long as he could patch up something, usually from stolen material, which would more or less hang together on the stage. However, that is not the whole story. To begin with, as Tolstoy himself points out, Shakespeare has a habit of thrusting uncalled-for general reflections into the mouths of his characters. This is a serious fault in a dramatist, but it does not fit in with Tolstoy's picture of Shakespeare as a vulgar hack who has no opinions of his own and merely wishes to produce the greatest effect with the least trouble. And more than this, about a dozen of his plays, written for the most part later than 1600, do unquestionably have a meaning and even a moral. They revolve round a central subject which in some cases can be reduced to a single word. For example, *Macbeth* is about ambition, *Othello* is about jealousy, and *Timon of Athens* is about money. The subject of *Lear* is renunciation, and it is only by being wilfully blind that one can fail to understand what Shakespeare is saying.

Lear renounces his throne but expects everyone to continue treating him as a king. He does not see that if he surrenders power, other people will take advantage of his weakness: also that those who flatter him the most grossly, i.e. Regan and Goneril, are exactly the ones who will turn against him. The moment he finds that he can no longer make people obey him as he did before, he falls into a rage which Tolstoy describes as "strange and unnatural," but which in fact is perfectly in character. In his madness and despair, he passes through two moods which again are natural enough in his circumstances, though in one of them it is probable that he is being used partly as a mouthpiece for Shakespeare's own opinions. One is the mood of disgust in which Lear repents, as it were, for having been a king, and grasps for the first time the rottenness of formal justice and vulgar morality. The other is a mood of impotent fury in which he wreaks imaginary revenges upon those who have wronged him. "To have a thousand with red burning spits come hissing in upon 'em!", and:

> It were a delicate stratagem to shoe
> A troop of horse with felt: I'll put't in proof;
> And when I have stol'n upon these sons-in-law,
> Then kill, kill, kill, kill, kill!

Only at the end does he realize, as a sane man, that power, revenge and victory are not worth while:

> No, no, no, no! Come, let's away to prison . . .
> . . . . and we'll wear out
> In a wall'd prison, packs and sects of great ones
> That ebb and flow by the moon.

But by the time he makes this discovery it is too late, for his death and Cordelia's are already decided on. That is the story, and, allowing for some clumsiness in the telling, it is a very good story.

But is it not also curiously similar to the history of Tolstoy himself? There is a general resemblance which one can hardly avoid seeing, because the most impressive event in Tolstoy's life, as in Lear's, was a huge and gratuitous act of renunciation. In his old age he renounced his estate, his title and his copyrights, and made an attempt—a sincere attempt, though it was not successful—to escape from his privileged position and live the life of a peasant. But the deeper resemblance lies in the fact that Tolstoy, like Lear, acted on mistaken motives and failed to get the results he had hoped for. According to Tolstoy, the aim of every human being is happiness, and happiness can only be attained by doing the will of God. But doing the will of God means casting off all earthly pleasures and ambitions, and living only for others. Ultimately, therefore, Tolstoy renounced the world under the expectation that this would make him happier. But if there is one thing certain about his later years, it is that he was *not* happy. On the contrary, he was driven almost to the edge of madness by the behavior of the people about him, who persecuted him precisely *because* of his renunciation. Like Lear, Tolstoy was not humble and not a good judge of character. He was inclined at moments to revert to the attitudes of an aristocrat, in spite of his peasant's blouse, and he even had two children whom he had believed in and who ultimately turned against him—though, of course, in a less sensational manner than Regan and Goneril. His exaggerated revulsion from sexuality was also distinctly similar to Lear's. Tolstoy's remark that marriage is "slavery, satiety, repulsion" and means putting up with the proximity of "ugliness, dirtiness, smell, sores," is matched by Lear's well-known outburst:

> But to the girdle do the gods inherit,
> Beneath is all the fiends';
> There's hell, there's darkness, there's the sulphurous pit,
> Burning, scalding, stench, consumption . . . etc., etc.

And though Tolstoy could not foresee it when he wrote his essay on Shakespeare, even the ending of his life—the sudden unplanned flight across country, accompanied only by a faithful daughter, the death in a cottage in a strange village—seems to have in it a sort of phantom reminiscence of *Lear*.

Of course, one cannot assume that Tolstoy was aware of this resemblance, or would have admitted it if it had been pointed out to him. But his attitude towards the play must have been influenced by its theme. Renouncing power, giving away your lands, was a subject on which he had reason to feel deeply. Probably, therefore, he would be more angered and disturbed by the moral that Shakespeare draws than he would be in the case of some other play—*Macbeth,* for example—which did not touch so closely on his own life. But what exactly *is* the moral of *Lear?* Evidently there are two morals, one explicit, the other implied in the story.

Shakespeare starts by assuming that to make yourself powerless is to invite an attack. This does not mean that *everyone* will turn against you (Kent and the Fool stand by Lear from first to last), but in all probability *someone* will. If you throw away your weapons, some less scrupulous person will pick them up. If you turn the other cheek, you will get a harder blow on it than you got on the first one. This does not always happen, but it is to be expected, and you ought not to complain if it does happen. The second blow is, so to speak, part of the act of turning the other cheek. First of all, therefore, there is the vulgar, common-sense moral drawn by the Fool: "Don't relinquish power, don't give away your lands." But there is also another moral. Shakespeare never utters it in so many words, and it does not very much matter whether he was fully aware of it. It is contained in the story, which, after all, he made up, or altered to suit his purposes. It is: "Give away your lands if you want to, but don't expect to gain happiness by doing so. Probably you won't gain happiness. If you live for others, you must live *for others,* and not as a roundabout way of getting an advantage for yourself."

Obviously neither of these conclusions could have been pleasing to Tolstoy. The first of them expresses the ordinary,

belly-to-earth selfishness from which he was genuinely trying
to escape. The other conflicts with his desire to eat his cake
and have it—that is, to destroy his own egoism and by so doing
to gain eternal life. Of course, *Lear* is not a sermon in favor
of altruism. It merely points out the results of practising self-
denial for selfish reasons. Shakespeare had a considerable
streak of worldliness in him, and if he had been forced to
take sides in his own play, his sympathies would probably have
lain with the Fool. But at least he could see the whole issue
and treat it at the level of tragedy. Vice is punished, but
virtue is not rewarded. The morality of Shakespeare's later
tragedies is not religious in the ordinary sense, and certainly
is not Christian. Only two of them, *Hamlet* and *Othello,* are
supposedly occurring inside the Christian era, and even in
those, apart from the antics of the ghost in *Hamlet,* there is
no indication of a "next world" where everything is to be
put right. All of these tragedies start out with the humanist
assumption that life, although full of sorrow, is worth living,
and that Man is a noble animal—a belief which Tolstoy in his
old age did not share.

Tolstoy was not a saint, but he tried very hard to make
himself into a saint, and the standards he applied to literature were other-worldly ones. It is important to realize that
the difference between a saint and an ordinary human being
is a difference of kind and not of degree. That is, the one is
not to be regarded as an imperfect form of the other. The
saint, at any rate Tolstoy's kind of saint, is not trying to work
an improvement in earthly life: he is trying to bring it to an
end and put something different in its place. One obvious
expression of this is the claim that celibacy is "higher" than
marriage. If only, Tolstoy says in effect, we would stop breeding, fighting, struggling and enjoying, if we could get rid not
only of our sins but of everything else that binds us to the

surface of the earth—including love, then the whole painful process would be over and the Kingdom of Heaven would
arrive. But a normal human being does not want the Kingdom of Heaven: he wants life on earth to continue. This is
not solely because he is "weak," "sinful" and anxious for a
"good time." Most people get a fair amount of fun out of
their lives, but on balance life is suffering, and only the very
young or the very foolish imagine otherwise. Ultimately it is
the Christian attitude which is self-interested and hedonistic,
since the aim is always to get away from the painful struggle
of earthly life and find eternal peace in some kind of Heaven
or Nirvana. The humanist attitude is that the struggle must
continue and that death is the price of life. "Men must endure
their going hence, even as their coming hither: Ripeness is
all"—which is an un-Christian sentiment. Often there is a
seeming truce between the humanist and the religious be-
liever, but in fact their attitudes cannot be reconciled: one
must choose between this world and the next. And the enormous majority of human beings, if they understood the issue,
would choose this world. They do make that choice when they
continue working, breeding and dying instead of crippling
their faculties in the hope of obtaining a new lease of existence elsewhere.

We do not know a great deal about Shakespeare's religious
beliefs, and from the evidence of his writings it would be difficult to prove that he had any. But at any rate he was not a
saint or a would-be saint: he was a human being, and in some
ways not a very good one. It is clear, for instance, that he liked
to stand well with the rich and powerful, and was capable of
flattering them in the most servile way. He is also noticeably
cautious, not to say cowardly, in his manner of uttering unpopular opinions. Almost never does he put a subversive or
sceptical remark into the mouth of a character likely to be

identified with himself. Throughout his plays the acute social
critics, the people who are not taken in by accepted fallacies,
are buffoons, villains, lunatics or persons who are shamming
insanity or are in a state of violent hysteria. *Lear* is a play in
which this tendency is particularly well marked. It contains
a great deal of veiled social criticism—a point Tolstoy misses—
but it is all uttered either by the Fool, by Edgar when he is
pretending to be mad, or by Lear during his bouts of madness. In his sane moments Lear hardly ever makes an intelligent remark. And yet the very fact that Shakespeare had to
use these subterfuges shows how widely his thoughts ranged.
He could not restrain himself from commenting on almost
everything, although he put on a series of masks in order to
do so. If one has once read Shakespeare with attention, it is
not easy to go a day without quoting him, because there are
not many subjects of major importance that he does not discuss or at least mention somewhere or other, in his unsystem-
atic but illuminating way. Even the irrelevancies that litter
every one of his plays—the puns and riddles, the lists of names,
the scraps of *reportage* like the conversation of the carriers in
Henry IV, the bawdy jokes, the rescued fragments of forgotten
ballads—are merely the products of excessive vitality. Shakespeare was not a philosopher or a scientist, but he did have
curiosity; he loved the surface of the earth and the process of
life—which, it should be repeated, is *not* the same thing as
wanting to have a good time and stay alive as long as possible. Of course, it is not because of the quality of his thought
that Shakespeare has survived, and he might not even be remembered as a dramatist if he had not also been a poet. His
main hold on us is through language. How deeply Shakespeare himself was fascinated by the music of words can probably be inferred from the speeches of Pistol. What Pistol says
is largely meaningless, but if one considers his lines singly

they are magnificent rhetorical verse. Evidently, pieces of resounding nonsense ("Let floods o'erswell, and fiends for food
howl on," etc.) were constantly appearing in Shakespeare's
mind of their own accord, and a half-lunatic character had to
be invented to use them up.

Tolstoy's native tongue was not English, and one cannot
blame him for being unmoved by Shakespeare's verse, nor
even, perhaps, for refusing to believe that Shakespeare's skill
with words was something out of the ordinary. But he would
also have rejected the whole notion of valuing poetry for its
texture—valuing it, that is to say, as a kind of music. If it
could somehow have been proved to him that his whole explanation of Shakespeare's rise to fame is mistaken, that inside
the English-speaking world, at any rate, Shakespeare's popularity is genuine, that his mere skill in placing one syllable
beside another has given acute pleasure to generation after
generation of English-speaking people—all this would not
have been counted as a merit to Shakespeare, but rather the
contrary. It would simply have been one more proof of the
irreligious, earthbound nature of Shakespeare and his admirers. Tolstoy would have said that poetry is to be judged
by its meaning, and that seductive sounds merely cause false
meanings to go unnoticed. At every level it is the same issue—
this world against the next: and certainly the music of words
is something that belongs to this world.

A sort of doubt has always hung around the character of
Tolstoy, as round the character of Gandhi. He was not a
vulgar hypocrite, as some people declared him to be, and he
would probably have imposed even greater sacrifices on himself than he did, if he had not been interfered with at every
step by the people surrounding him, especially his wife. But
on the other hand it is dangerous to take such men as Tolstoy
at their disciples' valuation. There is always the possibility—
the probability, indeed—that they have done no more than

exchange one form of egoism for another. Tolstoy renounced wealth, fame and privilege; he abjured violence in all its forms and was ready to suffer for doing so; but it is not easy to believe that he abjured the principle of coercion, or at least the *desire* to coerce others. There are families in which the father will say to his child, "You'll get a thick ear if you do that again," while the mother, her eyes brimming over with tears, will take the child in her arms and murmur lovingly, "Now, darling, *is* it kind to Mummy to do that?" And who would maintain that the second method is less tyrannous than the first? The distinction that really matters is not between violence and non-violence, but between having and not having the appetite for power. There are people who are convinced of the wickedness both of armies and of police forces, but who are nevertheless much more tolerant and inquisitorial in outlook than the normal person who believes that it is necessary to use violence in certain circumstances. They will not say to somebody else, "Do this, that and the other or you will go to prison," but they will, if they can, get inside his brain and dictate his thoughts for him in the minutest particulars. Creeds like pacifism and anarchism, which seem on the surface to imply a complete renunciation of power, rather encourage this habit of mind. For if you have embraced a creed which appears to be free from the ordinary dirtiness of politics—a creed from which you yourself cannot expect to draw any material advantage—surely that proves that you are in the right? And the more you are in the right, the more natural that everyone else should be bullied into thinking likewise.

If we are to believe what he says in his pamphlet, Tolstoy has never been able to see any merit in Shakespeare, and was always astonished to find that his fellow-writers, Turgenev, Fet and others thought differently. We may be sure that in his unregenerate days Tolstoy's conclusion would have been:

"You like Shakespeare—I don't. Let's leave it at that." Later, when his perception that it takes all sorts to make a world had deserted him, he came to think of Shakespeare's writings as something dangerous to himself. The more pleasure people took in Shakespeare, the less they would listen to Tolstoy. Therefore nobody must be *allowed* to enjoy Shakespeare, just as nobody must be allowed to drink alcohol or smoke tobacco. True, Tolstoy would not prevent them by force. He is not demanding that the police shall impound every copy of Shakespeare's works. But he will do dirt on Shakespeare, if he can. He will try to get inside the mind of every lover of Shakespeare and kill his enjoyment by every trick he can think of, including—as I have shown in my summary of his pamphlet—arguments which are self-contradictory or even doubtfully honest.

But finally the most striking thing is how little difference it all makes. As I said earlier, one cannot *answer* Tolstoy's pamphlet, at least on its main counts. There is no argument by which one can defend a poem. It defends itself by surviving, or it is indefensible. And if this test is valid, I think the verdict in Shakespeare's case must be "not guilty." Like every other writer, Shakespeare will be forgotten sooner or later, but it is unlikely that a heavier indictment will ever be brought against him. Tolstoy was perhaps the most admired literary man of his age, and he was certainly not its least able pamphleteer. He turned all his powers of denunciation against Shakespeare, like all the guns of a battleship roaring simultaneously. And with what result? Forty years later, Shakespeare is still there completely unaffected, and of the attempt to demolish him nothing remains except the yellowing pages of a pamphlet which hardly anyone has read, and which would be forgotten altogether if Tolstoy had not also been the author of *War and Peace* and *Anna Karenina*.

Politics vs. Literature:
an Examination of
"Gulliver's Travels"

IN "GULLIVER'S TRAVELS" HUMANITY IS ATTACKED, OR CRITICIZED, from at least three different angles, and the implied character of Gulliver himself necessarily changes somewhat in the process. In Part I he is the typical eighteenth-century voyager, bold, practical and unromantic, his homely outlook skilfully impressed on the reader by the biographical details at the beginning, by his age (he is a man of forty, with two children, when his adventures start), and by the inventory of the things in his pockets, especially his spectacles, which make several appearances. In Part II he has in general the same character, but at moments when the story demands it he has a tendency to develop into an imbecile who is capable of boasting of "our noble Country, the Mistress of Arts and Arms, the Scourge of France," etc., etc., and at the same time of betraying every available scandalous fact about the country which he professes to love. In Part III he is much as he was in Part I, though, as he is consorting chiefly with courtiers and men of learning, one has the impression that he has risen in the social scale. In Part IV he conceives a horror of the human race which is not apparent, or only intermittently apparent, in the earlier books, and changes into a sort of unreligious anchorite whose

one desire is to live in some desolate spot where he can devote
himself to meditating on the goodness of the Houyhnhnms.
However, these inconsistencies are forced upon Swift by the
fact that Gulliver is there chiefly to provide a contrast. It is
necessary, for instance, that he should appear sensible in
Part I and at least intermittently silly in Part II, because in
both books the essential maneuver is the same, i.e. to make
the human being look ridiculous by imagining him as a creature six inches high. Whenever Gulliver is not acting as a
stooge there is a sort of continuity in his character, which
comes out especially in his resourcefulness and his observation
of physical detail. He is much the same kind of person, with
the same prose style, when he bears off the warships of
Blefuscu, when he rips open the belly of the monstrous rat,
and when he sails away upon the ocean in his frail coracle
made from the skins of Yahoos. Moreover, it is difficult not to
feel that in his shrewder moments Gulliver is simply Swift
himself, and there is at least one incident in which Swift
seems to be venting his private grievance against contemporary Society. It will be remembered that when the Emperor
of Lilliput's palace catches fire, Gulliver puts it out by urinat-
ing on it. Instead of being congratulated on his presence of
mind, he finds that he has committed a capital offence by
making water in the precincts of the palace, and

I was privately assured, that the Empress, conceiving the greatest
Abhorrence of what I had done, removed to the most distant Side
of the Court, firmly resolved that those buildings should never be
repaired for her Use; and, in the Presence of her chief Confidents,
could not forbear vowing Revenge.

According to Professor G. M. Trevelyan (*England under
Queen Anne*), part of the reason for Swift's failure to get pre-
ferment was that the Queen was scandalized by the *Tale of a
Tub*—a pamphlet in which Swift probably felt that he had

done a great service to the English Crown, since it scarifies the Dissenters and still more the Catholics while leaving the Established Church alone. In any case no one would deny that *Gulliver's Travels* is a rancorous as well as a pessimistic book, and that especially in Parts I and III it often descends into political partisanship of a narrow kind. Pettiness and magnanimity, republicanism and authoritarianism, love of reason and lack of curiosity, are all mixed up in it. The hatred of the human body with which Swift is especially associated is only dominated in Part IV, but somehow this new preoccupation does not come as a surprise. One feels that all these adventures, and all these changes of mood, could have happened to the same person, and the inter-connection between Swift's political loyalties and his ultimate despair is one of the most interesting features of the book.

Politically, Swift was one of those people who are driven into a sort of perverse Toryism by the follies of the progressive party of the moment. Part I of *Gulliver's Travels*, ostensibly a satire on human greatness, can be seen, if one looks a little deeper, to be simply an attack on England, on the dominant Whig Party, and on the war with France, which—however bad the motives of the Allies may have been—did save Europe from being tyrannized over by a single reactionary power. Swift was not a Jacobite nor strictly speaking a Tory, and his declared aim in the war was merely a moderate peace treaty and not the outright defeat of England. Nevertheless there is a tinge of quislingism in his attitude, which comes out in the ending of Part I and slightly interferes with the allegory. When Gulliver flees from Lilliput (England) to Blefuscu (France) the assumption that a human being six inches high is inherently contemptible seems to be dropped. Whereas the people of Lilliput have behaved towards Gulliver with the utmost treachery and meanness, those of Blefuscu behave generously and straightforwardly, and indeed this section of the book ends on a different note from the all-round disillusionment of the earlier chapters. Evidently Swift's animus is, in the first place, against *England*. It is "your Natives" (i.e. Gulliver's fellow-countrymen) whom the King of Brobdingnag considers to be "the most pernicious Race of little odious vermin that Nature ever suffered to crawl upon the surface of the Earth," and the long passage at the end, denouncing colonization and foreign conquest, is plainly aimed at England, although the contrary is elaborately stated. The Dutch, England's allies and target of one of Swift's most famous pamphlets, are also more or less wantonly attacked in Part III. There is even what sounds like a personal note in the passage in which Gulliver records his satisfaction that the various countries he has discovered cannot be made colonies of the British Crown:

> The *Houyhnhnms,* indeed, appear not to be so well prepared for War, a Science to which they are perfect Strangers, and especially against missive Weapons. However, supposing myself to be a Minister of State, I could never give my advice for invading them. . . . Imagine twenty thousand of them breaking into the midst of an *European* army, confounding the Ranks, overturning the Carriages, battering the Warriors' Faces into Mummy, by terrible Yerks from their hinder hoofs. . . .

Considering that Swift does not waste words, that phrase, "battering the warriors' faces into mummy," probably indicates a secret wish to see the invincible armies of the Duke of Marlborough treated in a like manner. There are similar touches elsewhere. Even the country mentioned in Part III, where "the Bulk of the People consist, in a Manner, wholly of Discoverers, Witnesses, Informers, Accusers, Prosecutors, Evidences, Swearers, together with their several subservient and subaltern Instruments, all under the Colours, the Conduct, and Pay of Ministers of State," is called Langdon, which is within one letter of being an anagram of England. (As the early editions of the book contain misprints, it may perhaps have been intended as a complete anagram.) Swift's *physical* repulsion from humanity is certainly real enough, but one has the feeling that his debunking of human grandeur, his diatribes against lords, politicians, court favorites, etc., has mainly a local application and springs from the fact that he belonged to the unsuccessful party. He denounces injustice and oppression, but he gives no evidence of liking democracy. In spite of his enormously greater powers, his implied position is very similar to that of the innumerable silly-clever Conservatives of our own day—people like Sir Alan Herbert, Professor G. M. Young, Lord Elton, the Tory Reform Committee or the long line of Catholic apologists from W. H. Mallock onwards: people who specialize in cracking neat jokes at the expense of whatever is "modern" and "progressive," and whose opinions are often all the more extreme because they know that they cannot influence the actual drift of events. After all, such a pamphlet as *An Argument to prove that the Abolishing of Christianity*, etc., is very like "Timothy Shy" having a bit of clean fun with the Brains Trust, or Father Ronald Knox exposing the errors of Bertrand Russell. And the ease with which Swift has been forgiven—and forgiven, sometimes, by devout believers—for the blasphemies of *A Tale of a Tub* demonstrates clearly enough the feebleness of religious sentiments as compared with political ones.

However, the reactionary cast of Swift's mind does not show itself chiefly in his political affiliations. The important thing is his attitude towards Science, and, more broadly, towards intellectual curiosity. The famous Academy of Lagado, described in Part III of *Gulliver's Travels*, is no doubt a justified satire on most of the so-called scientists of Swift's own day. Significantly, the people at work in it are described as "Projectors," that is, people not engaged in disinterested research but merely on the look-out for gadgets which will save labor and bring in money. But there is no sign—indeed, all through the book there are many signs to the contrary—that "pure" science would have struck Swift as a worth-while activity. The more serious kind of scientist has already had a kick in the pants in Part II, when the "Scholars" patronized by the King of Brobdingnag try to account for Gulliver's small stature:

> After much Debate, they concluded unanimously that I was only *Relplum Scalcath*, which is interpreted literally, *Lusus Naturae;* a Determination exactly agreeable to the modern philosophy of *Europe*, whose Professors, disdaining the old Evasion of *Occult Causes*, whereby the followers of *Aristotle* endeavoured in vain to disguise their Ignorance, have invented this wonderful Solution of All Difficulties, to the unspeakable Advancement of human Knowledge.

If this stood by itself one might assume that Swift is merely the enemy of *sham* science. In a number of places, however, he goes out of his way to proclaim the uselessness of all learning or speculation not directed towards some practical end:

> The learning of [the Brobdingnagians] is very defective, consisting only in Morality, History, Poetry, and Mathematics, wherein they must be allowed to excel. But, the last of these is wholly applied to what may be useful in Life, to the improvement of Agriculture, and all mechanical Arts so that among us it would be little esteemed. And as to Ideas, Entities, Abstractions, and Transcendentals, I could never drive the least Conception into their Heads.

The Houyhnhnms, Swift's ideal beings, are backward even in a mechanical sense. They are unacquainted with metals, have never heard of boats, do not, properly speaking, practise agriculture (we are told that the oats which they live upon "grow naturally"), and appear not to have invented wheels.[1] They have no alphabet, and evidently have not much curiosity

---

[1] Houyhnhnms too old to walk are described as being carried in "sledges" or in "a kind of vehicle, drawn like a sledge." Presumably these had no wheels.

about the physical world. They do not believe that any in-
habited country exists beside their own, and though they
understand the motions of the sun and moon, and the nature
of eclipses, "this is the utmost progress of their *Astronomy*."
By contrast, the philosophers of the flying island of Laputa
are so continuously absorbed in mathematical speculations
that before speaking to them one has to attract their attention
by flapping them on the ear with a bladder. They have cata-
logued ten thousand fixed stars, have settled the periods of
ninety-three comets, and have discovered in advance of the
astronomers of Europe, that Mars has two moons—all of
which information Swift evidently regards as ridiculous, useless and uninteresting. As one might expect, he believes that
the scientist's place, if he has a place, is in the laboratory, and
that scientific knowledge has no bearing on political matters:

> What I . . . thought altogether unaccountable, was the strong Dis-
> position I observed in them towards News and Politics, perpetually
> enquiring into Public Affairs, giving their judgments in Matters of
> State, and passionately disputing every inch of a Party Opinion. I
> have, indeed, observed the same Disposition among most of the
> Mathematicians I have known in *Europe*, though I could never dis-
> cover the least Analogy between the two Sciences; unless those
> people suppose, that, because the smallest Circle hath as many De-
> grees as the largest, therefore the Regulation and Management of
> the World require no more Abilities, than the Handling and Turn-
> ing of a Globe.

Is there not something familiar in that phrase "I could never
discover the least analogy between the two sciences"? It has
precisely the note of the popular Catholic apologists who pro-
fess to be astonished when a scientist utters an opinion on
such questions as the existence of God or the immortality of
the soul. The scientist, we are told, is an expert only in one

restricted field: why should his opinions be of value in any other? The implication is that theology is just as much an exact science as, for instance, chemistry, and that the priest is also an expert whose conclusions on certain subjects must be accepted. Swift in effect makes the same claim for the politician, but he goes one better in that he will not allow the scientist—either the "pure" scientist or the *ad-hoc* investigator—to be a useful person in his own line. Even if he had not written Part III of *Gulliver's Travels,* one could infer from the rest of the book that, like Tolstoy and like Blake, he hates the very idea of studying the processes of Nature. The "Reason" which he so admires in the Houyhnhnms does not primarily mean the power of drawing logical inferences from observed facts. Although he never defines it, it appears in most contexts to mean either common sense—i.e. acceptance of the obvious and contempt for quibbles and abstractions— or absence of passion and superstition. In general he assumes that we know all that we need to know already, and merely use our knowledge incorrectly. Medicine, for instance, is a useless science, because if we lived in a more natural way, there would be no diseases. Swift, however, is not a simple-lifer or an admirer of the Noble Savage. He is in favor of civilization and the arts of civilization. Not only does he see the value of good manners, good conversation, and even learning of a literary and historical kind, he also sees that agriculture, navigation and architecture need to be studied and could with advantages be improved. But his implied aim is a static, incurious civilization—the world of his own day, a little cleaner, a little saner, with no radical change and no poking into the unknowable. More than one would expect in anyone so free from accepted fallacies, he reveres the past, especially classical antiquity, and believes that modern man has degenerated sharply during the past hundred years.[1] In the island of sorcerers, where the spirits of the dead can be called up at will:

> I desired that the Senate of *Rome* might appear before me in one large chamber, and a modern Representative in Counterview, in another. The first seemed to be an Assembly of Heroes and Demy-Gods, the other a Knot of Pedlars, Pick-pockets, Highwaymen and Bullies.

Although Swift uses this section of Part III to attack the truthfulness of recorded history, his critical spirit deserts him as soon as he is dealing with Greeks and Romans. He remarks, of course, upon the corruption of imperial Rome, but he has an almost unreasoning admiration for some of the leading figures of the ancient world:

> I was struck with profound Veneration at the sight of *Brutus,* and could easily discover the most consummate Virtue, the greatest Intrepidity and Firmness of Mind, the truest Love of his Country, and general Benevolence for Mankind, in every Lineament of his Countenance. . . . I had the honour to have much Conversation with *Brutus,* and was told, that his Ancestors *Junius, Socrates, Epaminondas, Cato* the younger, *Sir Thomas More,* and himself, were perpetually together: a *Sextumvirate,* to which all the Ages of the World cannot add a seventh.

It will be noticed that of these six people, only one is a Christian. This is an important point. If one adds together Swift's pessimism, his reverence for the past, his incuriosity and his horror of the human body, one arrives at an attitude common among religious reactionaries—that is, people who defend an unjust order of Society by claiming that this world cannot be substantially improved and only the "next world"

---

[1] The physical decadence which Swift claims to have observed may have been a reality at that date. He attributes it to syphilis, which was a new disease in Europe and may have been more virulent than it is now. Distilled liquors, also, were a novelty in the seventeenth century and must have led at first to a great increase in drunkenness.

matters. However, Swift shows no sign of having any religious beliefs, at least in any ordinary sense of the words. He does not appear to believe seriously in life after death, and his idea of goodness is bound up with republicanism, love of liberty, courage, "benevolence" (meaning in effect public spirit), "reason" and other pagan qualities. This reminds one that there is another strain in Swift, not quite congruous with his disbelief in progress and his general hatred of humanity.

To begin with, he has moments when he is "constructive" and even "advanced." To be occasionally inconsistent is almost a mark of vitality in Utopia books, and Swift sometimes inserts a word of praise into a passage that ought to be purely satirical. Thus, his ideas about the education of the young are fathered on to the Lilliputians, who have much the same views on this subject as the Houyhnhnms. The Lilliputians also have various social and legal institutions (for instance, there are old age pensions, and people are rewarded for keeping the law as well as punished for breaking it) which Swift would have liked to see prevailing in his own country. In the middle of this passage Swift remembers his satirical intention and adds, "In relating these and the following Laws, I would only be understood to mean the original Institutions, and not the most scandalous Corruptions into which these people are fallen by the degenerate Nature of Man": but as Lilliput is supposed to represent England, and the laws he is speaking of have never had their parallel in England, it is clear that the impulse to make constructive suggestions has been too much for him. But Swift's greatest contribution to political thought in the narrower sense of the words, is his attack especially in Part III, on what would now be called totalitarianism. He has an extraordinarily clear pre-vision of the spy-haunted "police State," with its endless heresy-hunts and treason trials, all really designed to neutralize popular discontent by changing it into war hysteria. And one must remember that Swift is here inferring the whole from a quite small part, for the feeble governments of his own day did not give him illustrations ready-made. For example, there is the professor at the School of Political Projectors who "shewed me a large Paper of Instructions for discovering Plots and Conspiracies," and who claimed that one can find people's secret thoughts by examining their excrement:

Because Men are never so serious, thoughtful, and intent, as when they are at Stool, which he found by frequent Experiment: for in such Conjunctures, when he used meerly as a trial to consider what was the best Way of murdering the King, his Ordure would have a tincture of Green; but quite different when he thought only of raising an Insurrection, or burning the Metropolis.

The professor and his theory are said to have been suggested to Swift by the—from our point of view—not particularly astonishing or disgusting fact that in a recent State trial some letters found in somebody's privy had been put in evidence. Later in the same chapter we seem to be positively in the middle of the Russian purges:

In the Kingdom of Tribnia, by the Natives called Langdon . . . the Bulk of the People consist, in a Manner, wholly of Discoverers, Witnesses, Informers, Accusers, Prosecutors, Evidences, Swearers. . . . It is first agreed, and settled among them, what suspected Persons shall be accused of a Plot: Then, effectual Care is taken to secure all their Letters and Papers, and put the Owners in Chains. These papers are delivered to a Sett of Artists, very dexterous in finding out the mysterious Meanings of Words, Syllables, and Letters. . . . Where this method fails, they have two others more effectual, which the Learned among them call *Acrostics* and *Anagrams. First,* they can decypher all initial Letters into political Meanings: Thus: N shall signify a Plot, B a Regiment of Horse, L a Fleet at Sea: Or, *Secondly,* by transposing the Letters of the Alphabet in any suspected Paper, they can lay open the deepest Designs of a discontented Party. So, for Example if I should say in a Letter to a Friend,

Our Brother Tom has just got the Piles, a skilful Decypherer would discover that the same Letters, which compose that Sentence, may be analysed in the following Words: *Resist—a Plot is brought Home— The Tour.*[1] And this is the anagrammatic method.

Other professors at the same school invent simplified languages, write books by machinery, educate their pupils by inscribing the lesson on a wafer and causing them to swallow it, or propose to abolish individuality altogether by cutting off part of the brain of one man and grafting it on to the head of another. There is something queerly familiar in the atmosphere of these chapters, because, mixed up with much fooling, there is a perception that one of the aims of totalitarianism is not merely to make sure that people will think the right thoughts, but actually to make them *less conscious.* Then, again, Swift's account of the Leader who is usually to be found ruling over a tribe of Yahoos, and of the "favorite" who acts first as a dirty-worker and later as a scapegoat, fits remarkably well into the pattern of our own times. But are we to infer from all this that Swift was first and foremost an enemy of tyranny and a champion of the free intelligence? No: his own views, so far as one can discern them, are not markedly liberal. No doubt he hates lords, kings, bishops, generals, ladies of fashion, orders, titles and flummery generally, but he does not seem to think better of the common people than of their rulers, or to be in favor of increased social equality, or to be enthusiastic about representative institutions. The Houyhnhnms are organized upon a sort of caste system which is racial in character, the horses which do the menial work being of different colors from their masters and not interbreeding with them. The educational system which Swift admires in the Lilliputians takes hereditary class distinctions for granted, and the children of the poorest classes do not go to

[1] Tower.

school, because "their Business being only to till and cultivate the Earth . . . therefore their Education is of little Conse-quence to the Public." Nor does he seem to have been strongly in favor of freedom of speech and the Press, in spite of the toleration which his own writings enjoyed. The King of Brob-dingnag is astonished at the multiplicity of religious and po-litical sects in England, and considers that those who hold "opinions prejudicial to the public" (in the context this seems to mean simply heretical opinions), though they need not be obliged to change them, ought to be obliged to conceal them: for "as it was Tyranny in any Government to require the first, so it was weakness not to enforce the second." There is a sub-tler indication of Swift's own attitude in the manner in which Gulliver leaves the land of the Houyhnhnms. Intermittently, at least, Swift was a kind of anarchist, and Part IV of *Gulli-ver's Travels* is a picture of an anarchistic Society, not governed by law in the ordinary sense, but by the dictates of "Reason," which are voluntarily accepted by everyone. The General As-sembly of the Houyhnhnms "exhorts" Gulliver's master to get rid of him, and his neighbors put pressure on him to make him comply. Two reasons are given. One is that the presence of this unusual Yahoo may unsettle the rest of the tribe, and the other is that a friendly relationship between a Houyhn-hnm and a Yahoo is "not agreeable to Reason or Nature, or a Thing ever heard of before among them." Gulliver's mas-ter is somewhat unwilling to obey, but the "exhortation" (a Houyhnhnm, we are told, is never *compelled* to do anything, he is merely "exhorted" or "advised") cannot be disregarded. This illustrates very well the totalitarian tendency which is explicit in the anarchist or pacifist vision of Society. In a So-ciety in which there is no law, and in theory no compulsion, the only arbiter of behavior is public opinion. But public opinion, because of the tremendous urge to conformity in gregarious animals, is less tolerant than any system of law. When human beings are governed by "thou shalt not," the individual can practise a certain amount of eccentricity: when they are supposedly governed by "love" or "reason," he is under continuous pressure to make him behave and think in exactly the same way as everyone else. The Houyhnhnms, we are told, were unanimous on almost all subjects. The only question they ever *discussed* was how to deal with the Yahoos. Otherwise there was no room for disagreement among them, because the truth is always either self-evident, or else it is undiscoverable and unimportant. They had apparently no word for "opinion" in their language, and in their conversations there was no "difference of sentiments." They had reached, in fact, the highest stage of totalitarian organization, the stage when conformity has become so general that there is no need for a police force. Swift approves of this kind of thing because among his many gifts neither curiosity nor good-nature was included. Disagreement would always seem to him sheer perversity. "Reason," among the Houyhnhnms, he says, "is not a Point Problematical, as with us, where men can argue with Plausibility on both Sides of a Question; but strikes you with immediate Conviction; as it must needs do, where it is not mingled, obscured, or discoloured by Passion and Interest." In other words, we know everything already, so why should dissident opinions be tolerated? The totalitarian Society of the Houyhnhnms, where there can be no freedom and no development, follows naturally from this.

We are right to think of Swift as a rebel and iconoclast, but except in certain secondary matters, such as his insistence that women should receive the same education as men, he cannot be labelled "Left." He is a Tory anarchist, despising authority while disbelieving in liberty, and preserving the aristocratic outlook while seeing clearly that the existing aristocracy is degenerate and contemptible. When Swift utters one of his characteristic diatribes against the rich and powerful, one must probably, as I said earlier, write off something for the fact that he himself belonged to the less successful party, and was personally disappointed. The "outs," for obvious reasons, are always more radical than the "ins." [1] But the most essential thing in Swift is his inability to believe that life—ordinary life on the solid earth, and not some rationalized, deodorized version of it—could be made worth living. Of course, no honest person claims that happiness is *now* a normal condition among adult human beings; but perhaps it *could* be made normal, and it is upon this question that all serious political controversy really turns. Swift has much in common—more, I believe, than has been noticed—with Tolstoy, another disbeliever in the possibility of happiness. In both men you have the same anarchistic outlook covering an authoritarian cast of mind; in both a similar hostility to Science, the same impatience with opponents, the same inability to see the importance of any question not interesting to themselves; and in both cases a sort of horror of the actual process of life, though in Tolstoy's case it was arrived at later and in a different way. The sexual unhappiness of the two men was not of the same kind, but there was this in common, that in both of them a sincere loathing was mixed up with a morbid

[1] At the end of the book, as typical specimens of human folly and viciousness, Swift names "a Lawyer, a Pickpocket, a Colonel, a Fool, a Lord, a Gamester, a Politician, a Whore-master, a Physician, an Evidence, a Suborner, an Attorney, a Traitor, or the like." One sees here the irresponsible violence of the powerless. The list lumps together those who break the conventional code, and those who keep it. For instance, if you automatically condemn a colonel, as such, on what grounds do you condemn a traitor? Or again, if you want to suppress pickpockets, you must have laws, which means that you must have lawyers. But the whole closing passage, in which the hatred is so authentic, and the reason given for it so inadequate, is somehow unconvincing. One has the feeling that personal animosity is at work.

fascination. Tolstoy was a reformed rake who ended by preaching complete celibacy, while continuing to practise the opposite into extreme old age. Swift was presumably impotent, and had an exaggerated horror of human dung: he also thought about it incessantly, as is evident throughout his works. Such people are not likely to enjoy even the small amount of happiness that falls to most human beings and, from obvious motives, are not likely to admit that earthly life is capable of much improvement. Their incuriosity, and hence their intolerance, spring from the same root.

Swift's disgust, rancor and pessimism would make sense against the background of a "next world" to which this one is the prelude. As he does not appear to believe seriously in any such thing, it becomes necessary to construct a paradise supposedly existing on the surface of the earth, but something quite different from anything we know, with all that he disapproves of—lies, folly, change, enthusiasm, pleasure, love and dirt—eliminated from it. As his ideal being he chooses the horse, an animal whose excrement is not offensive. The Houyhnhnms are dreary beasts—this is so generally admitted that the point is not worth laboring. Swift's genius can make them credible, but there can have been very few readers in whom they have excited any feeling beyond dislike. And this is not from wounded vanity at seeing animals preferred to men; for, of the two, the Houyhnhnms are much liker to human beings than are the Yahoos, and Gulliver's horror of the Yahoos, together with his recognition that they are the same kind of creature as himself, contains a logical absurdity. This horror comes upon him at his very first sight of them. "I never beheld," he says, "in all my Travels, so disagreeable an Animal, nor one against which I naturally conceived so strong an Antipathy." But in comparison with what are the Yahoos disgusting? Not with the Houyhnhnms, because at this time Gul-

liver has not seen a Houyhnhnm. It can only be in comparison
with himself, i.e. with a human being. Later, however, we are
to be told that the Yahoos *are* human beings, and human society becomes insupportable to Gulliver because all men are
Yahoos. In that case why did he not conceive his disgust of
humanity earlier? In effect we are told that the Yahoos are
fantastically different from men, and yet are the same. Swift
has over-reached himself in his fury, and is shouting at his
fellow-creatures: "You are filthier than you are!" However, it
is impossible to feel much sympathy with the Yahoos, and it
is not because they oppress the Yahoos that the Houyhnhnms
are unattractive. They are unattractive because the "Reason"
by which they are governed is really a desire for death. They
are exempt from love, friendship, curiosity, fear, sorrow and—
except in their feelings towards the Yahoos, who occupy rather
the same place in their community as the Jews in Nazi Germany—anger and hatred. "They have no Fondness for their
Colts or Foles, but the Care they take, in educating them, proceeds entirely from the Dictates of *Reason.*" They lay store
by "Friendship" and "Benevolence," but "these are not confined to particular Objects, but universal to the whole Race."
They also value conversation, but in their conversations
there are no differences of opinion, and "nothing passed
but what was useful, expressed in the fewest and most significant Words." They practise strict birth control, each
couple producing two offspring and thereafter abstaining
from sexual intercourse. Their marriages are arranged for
them by their elders, on eugenic principles, and their language contains no word for "love," in the sexual sense. When
somebody dies they carry on exactly as before, without feeling
any grief. It will be seen that their aim is to be as like a corpse
as is possible while retaining physical life. One or two of their
characteristics, it is true, do not seem to be strictly "reasonable"

in their own usage of the word. Thus, they place a great value
not only on physical hardihood but on athleticism, and they
are devoted to poetry. But these exceptions may be less arbitrary than they seem. Swift probably emphasizes the physical
strength of the Houyhnhnms in order to make clear that they
could never be conquered by the hated human race, while a
taste for poetry may figure among their qualities because
poetry appeared to Swift as the antithesis of Science, from his
point of view the most useless of all pursuits. In Part III he
names "Imagination, Fancy, and Invention" as desirable faculties in which the Laputan mathematicians (in spite of their
love of music) were wholly lacking. One must remember that
although Swift was an admirable writer of comic verse, the
kind of poetry he thought valuable would probably be didactic
poetry. The poetry of the Houyhnhnms, he says—

> must be allowed to excel (that of) all other Mortals; wherein the
> Justness of their Similes, and the Minuteness, as well as exactness,
> of their Descriptions, are, indeed, inimitable. Their Verses abound
> very much in both of these; and usually contain either some exalted
> Notions of Friendship and Benevolence, or the Praises of those who
> were Victors in Races, and other bodily Exercises.

Alas, not even the genius of Swift was equal to producing a
specimen by which we could judge the poetry of the Houyhnhnms. But it sounds as though it were chilly stuff (in heroic
couplets, presumably), and not seriously in conflict with the
principles of "Reason."

Happiness is notoriously difficult to describe, and pictures
of a just and well-ordered Society are seldom either attractive
or convincing. Most creators of "favorable" Utopias, however,
are concerned to show what life could be like if it were lived
more fully. Swift advocates a simple refusal of life, justifying
this by the claim that "Reason" consists in thwarting your
instincts. The Houyhnhnms, creatures without a history, con-

tinue for generation after generation to live prudently, main-
taining their population at exactly the same level, avoiding
all passion, suffering from no diseases, meeting death indifferently, training up their young in the same principles—and
all for what? In order that the same process may continue
indefinitely. The notions that life here and now is worth living, or that it could be made worth living, or that it must be
sacrificed for some future good, are all absent. The dreary
world of the Houyhnhnms was about as good a Utopia as Swift
could construct, granting that he neither believed in a "next
world" nor could get any pleasure out of certain normal activities. But it is not really set up as something desirable in itself,
but as the justification for another attack on humanity. The
aim, as usual, is to humiliate Man by reminding him that he is
weak and ridiculous, and above all that he stinks; and the ultimate motive, probably, is a kind of envy, the envy of the ghost
for the living, of the man who knows he cannot be happy for
the others who—so he fears—may be a little happier than himself. The political expression of such an outlook must be either
reactionary or nihilistic, because the person who holds it will
want to prevent Society from developing in some direction in
which his pessimism may be cheated. One can do this either by
blowing everything to pieces, or by averting social change.
Swift ultimately blew everything to pieces in the only way that
was feasible before the atomic bomb—that is, he went mad—
but, as I have tried to show, his political aims were on the
whole reactionary ones.

From what I have written it may have seemed that I am
against Swift, and that my object is to refute him and even to
belittle him. In a political and moral sense I am against him,
so far as I understand him. Yet curiously enough he is one of
the writers I admire with least reserve, and *Gulliver's Travels*,
in particular, is a book which it seems impossible for me to

grow tired of. I read it first when I was eight—one day short
of eight, to be exact, for I stole and furtively read the copy
which was to be given me next day on my eighth birthday—
and I have certainly not read it less than half a dozen times
since. Its fascination seems inexhaustible. If I had to make a
list of six books which were to be preserved when all others
were destroyed, I would certainly put *Gulliver's Travels*
among them. This raises the question: what is the relationship
between agreement with a writer's opinions, and enjoyment
of his work?

If one is capable of intellectual detachment, one can *per-
ceive* merit in a writer whom one deeply disagrees with, but
enjoyment is a different matter. Supposing that there is such
a thing as good or bad art, then the goodness or badness must
reside in the work of art itself—not independently of the observer, indeed, but independently of the mood of the observer.
In one sense, therefore, it cannot be true that a poem is good
on Monday and bad on Tuesday. But if one judges the poem
by the appreciation it arouses, then it can certainly be true,
because appreciation or enjoyment is a subjective condition
which cannot be commanded. For a great deal of his waking
life, even the most cultivated person has no aesthetic feelings
whatever, and the power to have aesthetic feelings is very easily
destroyed. When you are frightenend, or hungry, or are suffering from toothache or sea-sickness, *King Lear* is no better
from your point of view than *Peter Pan*. You may know in an
intellectual sense that it is better, but that is simply a fact
which you remember: you will not *feel* the merit of *King Lear*
until you are normal again. And aesthetic judgment can be up-
set just as disastrously—more disastrously, because the cause is
no less readily recognized—by political or moral disagreement.
If a book angers, wounds or alarms you, then you will not
enjoy it, whatever its merits may be. If it seems to you a really

pernicious book, likely to influence other people in some undesirable way, then you will probably construct an aesthetic
theory to show that it *has* no merits. Current literary criticism
consists quite largely of this kind of dodging to and fro between two sets of standards. And yet the opposite process can
also happen: enjoyment can overwhelm disapproval, even
though one clearly recognizes that one is enjoying something
inimical. Swift, whose world-view is so peculiarly unaccept-
able, but who is nevertheless an extremely popular writer, is
a good instance of this. Why is it that we don't mind being
called Yahoos, although firmly convinced that we are *not*
Yahoos?

It is not enough to make the usual answer that of course
Swift was wrong, in fact he was insane, but he was "a good
writer." It is true that the literary quality of a book is to some
small extent separable from its subject-matter. Some people
have a native gift for using words, as some people have a naturally "good eye" at games. It is largely a question of timing
and of instinctively knowing how much emphasis to use. As
an example near at hand, look back at the passage I quoted
earlier, starting "In the Kingdom of Tribnia, by the Natives
called Langdon." It derives much of its force from the final
sentence: "And this is the anagrammatic Method." Strictly
speaking this sentence is unnecessary, for we have already seen
the anagram decyphered, but the mock-solemn repetition, in
which one seems to hear Swift's own voice uttering the words,
drives home the idiocy of the activities described, like the final
tap to a nail. But not all the power and simplicity of Swift's
prose, nor the imaginative effort that has been able to make
not one but a whole series of impossible worlds more credible
than the majority of history books—none of this would enable
us to enjoy Swift if his world-view were truly wounding or
shocking. Millions of people, in many countries, must have

enjoyed *Gulliver's Travels* while more or less seeing its anti-human implications: and even the child who accepts Parts I and II as a simple story gets a sense of absurdity from thinking of human beings six inches high. The explanation must be that Swift's world-view is felt to be *not* altogether false—or it would probably be more accurate to say, not false all the time. Swift is a diseased writer. He remains permanently in a depressed mood which in most people is only intermittent, rather as though someone suffering from jaundice or the after-effects of influenza should have the energy to write books. But we all know that mood, and something in us responds to the expression of it. Take, for instance, one of his most characteristic works, *The Lady's Dressing Room:* one might add the kindred poem, *Upon a Beautiful Young Nymph Going to Bed.* Which is truer, the viewpoint expressed in these poems, or the viewpoint implied in Blake's phrase, "The naked female human form divine"? No doubt Blake is nearer the truth, and yet who can fail to feel a sort of pleasure in seeing that fraud, feminine delicacy, exploded for once? Swift falsifies his picture of the world by refusing to see anything in human life except dirt, folly and wickedness, but the part which he abstracts from the whole does exist, and it is something which we all know about while shrinking from mentioning it. Part of our minds—in any normal person it is the dominant part—believes that man is a noble animal and life is worth living: but there is also a sort of inner self which at least intermittently stands aghast at the horror of existence. In the queerest way, pleasure and disgust are linked together. The human body is beautiful: it is also repulsive and ridiculous, a fact which can be verified at any swimming pool. The sexual organs are objects of desire and also of loathing, so much so that in many languages, if not in all languages, their names are used as words of abuse. Meat is delicious, but a butcher's shop makes one feel sick: and indeed all our food springs ultimately from dung and dead bodies, the two things which of all others seem to us the most horrible. A child, when it is past the infantile stage but still looking at the world with fresh eyes, is moved by horror almost as often as by wonder—horror of snot and spittle, of the dogs' excrement on the pavement, the dying toad full of maggots, the sweaty smell of grown-ups, the hideousness of old men, with their bald heads and bulbous noses. In his endless harping on disease, dirt and deformity, Swift is not actually inventing anything, he is merely leaving something out. Human behavior, too, especially in politics, is as he describes it, although it contains other more important factors which he refuses to admit. So far as we can see, both horror and pain are necessary to the continuance of life on this planet, and it is therefore open to pessimists like Swift to say: "If horror and pain must always be with us, how can life be significantly improved?" His attitude is in effect the Christian attitude, minus the bribe of a "next world"—which, however, probably has less hold upon the minds of believers than the conviction that this world is a vale of tears and the grave is a place of rest. It is, I am certain, a wrong attitude, and one which could have harmful effects upon behavior; but something in us responds to it, as it responds to the gloomy words of the burial service and the sweetish smell of corpses in a country church.

It is often argued, at least by people who admit the importance of subject-matter, that a book cannot be "good" if it expresses a palpably false view of life. We are told that in our own age, for instance, any book that has genuine literary merit will also be more or less "progressive" in tendency. This ignores the fact that throughout history a similar struggle between progress and reaction has been raging, and that the best books of any one age have always been written from several different viewpoints, some of them palpably more false than others. In so far as a writer is a propagandist, the most one can ask of him is that he shall genuinely believe in what he is saying, and that it shall not be something blazingly silly. Today, for example, one can imagine a good book being written by a Catholic, a Communist, a Fascist, a pacifist, an anarchist, perhaps by an old-style Liberal or an ordinary Conservative: one cannot imagine a good book being written by a spiritualist, a Buchmanite or a member of the Ku Klux Klan. The views that a writer holds must be compatible with sanity, in the medical sense, and with the power of continuous thought: beyond that what we ask of him is talent, which is probably another name for conviction. Swift did not possess ordinary wisdom, but he did possess a terrible intensity of vision, capable of picking out a single hidden truth and then magnifying it and distorting it. The durability of *Gulliver's Travels* goes to show that, if the force of belief is behind it, a world-view which only just passes the test of sanity is sufficient to produce a great work of art.

Politics and the English Language

MOST PEOPLE WHO BOTHER WITH THE MATTER AT ALL WOULD admit that the English language is in a bad way, but it is generally assumed that we cannot by conscious action do anything about it. Our civilization is decadent and our language—so the argument runs—must inevitably share in the general collapse. It follows that any struggle against the abuse of language is a sentimental archaism, like preferring candles to electric light or hansom cabs to aeroplanes. Underneath this lies the half-conscious belief that language is a natural growth and not an instrument which we shape for our own purposes.

Now, it is clear that the decline of a language must ultimately have political and economic causes: it is not due simply to the bad influence of this or that individual writer. But an effect can become a cause, reinforcing the original cause and producing the same effect in an intensified form, and so on indefinitely. A man may take to drink because he feels himself to be a failure, and then fail all the more completely because he drinks. It is rather the same thing that is happening to the English language. It becomes ugly and inaccurate because our thoughts are foolish, but the slovenliness of our language makes it easier for us to have foolish thoughts. The point is that the process is reversible. Modern English, especially written English, is full of bad habits which spread by imitation and which can be avoided if one is willing to take the necessary trouble. If one gets rid of these habits one can think more clearly, and to think clearly is a necessary first step towards political regeneration: so that the fight against bad English is not frivolous and is not the exclusive concern of professional writers. I will come back to this presently, and I hope that by that time the meaning of what I have said here will have become clearer. Meanwhile, here are five specimens of the English language as it is now habitually written.

These five passages have not been picked out because they are especially bad—I could have quoted far worse if I had chosen—but because they illustrate various of the mental vices from which we now suffer. They are a little below the average, but are fairly representative samples. I number them so that I can refer back to them when necessary:

(1) I am not, indeed, sure whether it is not true to say that the Milton who once seemed not unlike a seventeenth-century Shelley had not become, out of an experience ever more bitter in each year, more alien [sic] to the founder of that Jesuit sect which nothing could induce him to tolerate.

Professor Harold Laski
(Essay in *Freedom of Expression*).

(2) Above all, we cannot play ducks and drakes with a native battery of idioms which prescribes such egregious collocations of vocables as the Basic *put up with* for *tolerate* or *put at a loss* for *bewilder*.

Professor Lancelot Hogben (*Interglossa*).

(3) On the one side we have the free personality: by definition it is not neurotic, for it has neither conflict nor dream. Its desires, such as they are, are transparent, for they are just what institutional approval keeps in the forefront of consciousness; another institutional pattern would alter their number and intensity; there is little in them that is natural, irreducible, or culturally dangerous. But *on the other side,* the social bond itself is nothing but the mutual reflection of these self-secure integrities. Recall the definition of love. Is not this the very picture of a small academic? Where is there a place in this hall of mirrors for either personality or fraternity?

Essay on psychology in *Politics* (New York).

(4) All the "best people" from the gentlemen's clubs, and all the frantic fascist captains, united in common hatred of Socialism and bestial horror of the rising tide of the mass revolutionary movement, have turned to acts of provocation, to foul incendiarism, to medieval legends of poisoned wells, to legalize their own destruction of proletarian organizations, and rouse the agitated petty-bourgeoisie to chauvinistic fervor on behalf of the fight against the revolutionary way out of the crisis.

                                                    Communist pamphlet.

(5) If a new spirit *is* to be infused into this old country, there is one thorny and contentious reform which must be tackled, and that is the humanization and galvanization of the B.B.C. Timidity here will bespeak canker and atrophy of the soul. The heart of Britain may be sound and of strong beat, for instance, but the British lion's roar at present is like that of Bottom in Shakespeare's *Midsummer Night's Dream*—as gentle as any sucking dove. A virile new Britain cannot continue indefinitely to be traduced in the eyes or rather ears, of the world by the effete languors of Langham Place, brazenly masquerading as "standard English." When the Voice of Britain is heard at nine o'clock, better far and infinitely less ludicrous to hear aitches honestly dropped than the present priggish, inflated, inhibited, school-ma'amish arch braying of blameless bashful mewing maidens!

                                                    Letter in *Tribune*

Each of these passages has faults of its own, but, quite apart from avoidable ugliness, two qualities are common to all of them. The first is staleness of imagery; the other is lack of precision. The writer either has a meaning and cannot express it, or he inadvertently says something else, or he is almost indifferent as to whether his words mean anything or not. This mixture of vagueness and sheer incompetence is the most marked characteristic of modern English prose, and especially of any kind of political writing. As soon as certain topics are raised, the concrete melts into the abstract and no one seems able to think of turns of speech that are not hackneyed: prose consists less and less of *words* chosen for the sake of their meaning, and more and more of *phrases* tacked together like the sections of a prefabricated hen-house. I list below, with notes and examples, various of the tricks by means of which the work of prose-construction is habitually dodged:

Dying metaphors. A newly invented metaphor assists thought by evoking a visual image, while on the other hand a metaphor which is technically "dead" (e.g. *iron resolution*) has in effect reverted to being an ordinary word and can generally be used without loss of vividness. But in between these two classes there is a huge dump of worn-out metaphors which have lost all evocative power and are merely used because they save people the trouble of inventing phrases for themselves. Examples are: *Ring the changes on, take up the cudgels for, toe the line, ride roughshod over, stand shoulder to shoulder with, play into the hands of, no axe to grind, grist to the mill, fishing in troubled waters, on the order of the day, Achilles' heel, swan song, hotbed.* Many of these are used without knowledge of their meaning (what is a "rift," for instance?), and incompatible metaphors are frequently mixed, a sure sign that the writer is not interested in what he is saying. Some metaphors now current have been twisted out of their original meaning without those who use them even being aware of the fact. For example, *toe the line* is sometimes written *tow the line.* Another example is *the hammer and the anvil,* now always used with the implication that the anvil gets the worst of it. In real life it is always the anvil that breaks the hammer, never the other way about: a writer who stopped to think what he was saying would be aware of this, and would avoid perverting the original phrase.

Operators or *verbal false limbs.* These save the trouble of picking out appropriate verbs and nouns, and at the same time pad each sentence with extra syllables which give it an appearance of symmetry. Characteristic phrases are *render inopera-*

tive, militate against, make contact with, be subjected to, give rise to, give grounds for, have the effect of, play a leading part (role) in, make itself felt, take effect, exhibit a tendency to, serve the purpose of, etc., etc. The keynote is the elimination of simple verbs. Instead of being a single word, such as *break, stop, spoil, mend, kill,* a verb becomes a *phrase,* made up of a noun or adjective tacked on to some general-purposes verb such as *prove, serve, form, play, render.* In addition, the passive voice is wherever possible used in preference to the active, and noun constructions are used instead of gerunds (*by examination of* instead of *by examining*). The range of verbs is further cut down by means of the *-ize* and *de-* formations, and the banal statements are given an appearance of profundity by means of the *not un-* formation. Simple conjunctions and prepositions are replaced by such phrases as *with respect to, having regard to, the fact that, by dint of, in view of, in the interests of, on the hypothesis that;* and the ends of sentences are saved by anticlimax by such resounding common-places as *greatly to be desired, cannot be left out of account, a development to be expected in the near future, deserving of serious consideration, brought to a satisfactory conclusion,* and so on and so forth.

Pretentious diction. Words like *phenomenon, element, individual* (as noun), *objective, categorical, effective, virtual, basic, primary, promote, constitute, exhibit, exploit, utilize, eliminate, liquidate,* are used to dress up simple statement and give an air of scientific impartiality to biased judgments. Adjectives like *epoch-making, epic, historic, unforgettable, triumphant, age-old, inevitable, inexorable, veritable,* are used to dignify the sordid processes of international politics, while writing that aims at glorifying war usually takes on an archaic color, its characteristic words being: *realm, throne, chariot, mailed fist, trident, sword, shield, buckler, banner, jackboot,*

clarion. Foreign words and expressions such as *cul de sac,
ancien régime, deus ex machina, mutatis mutandis, status quo,
gleichschaltung, weltanschauung,* are used to give an air of
culture and elegance. Except for the useful abbreviations *i.e.,
e.g.,* and *etc.,* there is no real need for any of the hundreds of
foreign phrases now current in English. Bad writers, and especially scientific, political and sociological writers, are nearly
always haunted by the notion that Latin or Greek words are
grander than Saxon ones, and unnecessary words like *expedite,
ameliorate, predict, extraneous, deracinated, clandestine, sub-
aqueous* and hundreds of others constantly gain ground from
their Anglo-Saxon opposite numbers.[1] The jargon peculiar to
Marxist writing *(hyena, hangman, cannibal, petty bourgeois,
these gentry, lacquey, flunkey, mad dog, White Guard,* etc.)
consists largely of words and phrases translated from Russian,
German or French; but the normal way of coining a new
word is to use a Latin or Greek root with the appropriate
affix and, where necessary, the size formation. It is often easier
to make up words of this kind *(deregionalize, impermissible,
extramarital, non-fragmentary* and so forth) than to think
up the English words that will cover one's meaning. The result, in general, is an increase in slovenliness and vagueness.

Meaningless words. In certain kinds of writing, particularly
in art criticism and literary criticism, it is normal to come
across long passages which are almost completely lacking in
meaning.[2] Words like *romantic, plastic, values, human, dead,*

---

[1] An interesting illustration of this is the way in which the English flower
names which were in use till very recently are being ousted by Greek ones,
snapdragon becoming *antirrhinum, forget-me-not* becoming *myosotis,* etc.
It is hard to see any practical reason for this change of fashion: it is probably due to an instinctive turning-away from the more homely word and
a vague feeling that the Greek word is scientific.

[2] Example: "Comfort's catholicity of perception and image, strangely
Whitmanesque in range, almost the exact opposite in aesthetic compulsion,
continues to evoke that trembling atmospheric accumulative hinting at a
cruel, an inexorably serene timelessness. . . . Wrey Gardiner scores by aim-

sentimental, natural, vitality, as used in art criticism, are strictly meaningless, in the sense that they not only do not point to any discoverable object, but are hardly ever expected to do so by the reader. When one critic writes, "The outstanding feature of Mr. X's work is its living quality," while another writes, "The immediately striking thing about Mr. X's work is its peculiar deadness," the reader accepts this as a simple difference of opinion. If words like *black* and *white* were involved, instead of the jargon words *dead* and *living,* he would see at once that language was being used in an improper way. Many political words are similarly abused. The word *Fascism* has now no meaning except in so far as it signifies "something not desirable." The words *democracy, socialism, freedom, patriotic, realistic, justice,* have each of them several different meanings which cannot be reconciled with one another. In the case of a word like *democracy,* not only is there no agreed definition, but the attempt to make one is resisted from all sides. It is almost universally felt that when we call a country democratic we are praising it: consequently the defenders of every kind of régime claim that it is a democracy, and fear that they might have to stop using the word if it were tied down to any one meaning. Words of this kind are often used in a consciously dishonest way. That is, the person who uses them has his own private definition, but allows his hearer to think he means something quite different. Statements like *Marshal Pétain was a true patriot, The Soviet Press is the freest in the world, The Catholic Church is opposed to persecution,* are almost always made with intent to deceive. Other words used in variable meanings, in most cases more or less dishonestly, are: *class, totalitarian, science, progressive, reactionary, bourgeois, equality.*

ing at simple bull's-eyes with precision. Only they are not so simple, and through this contented sadness runs more than the surface bitter-sweet of resignation." (*Poetry Quarterly.*)

Now that I have made this catalogue of swindles and per-
versions, let me give another example of the kind of writing
that they lead to. This time it must of its nature be an imaginary one. I am going to translate a passage of good English
into modern English of the worst sort. Here is a well-known
verse from *Ecclesiastes:*

"I returned and saw under the sun, that the race is not to
the swift, nor the battle to the strong, neither yet bread to
the wise, nor yet riches to men of understanding, nor yet
favour to men of skill; but time and chance happeneth to
them all."

Here it is in modern English:

"Objective considerations of contemporary phenomena compels the conclusion that success or failure in competitive activities exhibits no tendency to be commensurate with innate ca-
pacity, but that a considerable element of the unpredictable
must invariably be taken into account."

This is a parody, but not a very gross one. Exhibit (3),
above, for instance, contains several patches of the same kind
of English. It will be seen that I have not made a full translation. The beginning and ending of the sentence follow the
original meaning fairly closely, but in the middle the concrete illustrations—race, battle, bread—dissolve into the vague
phrase "success or failure in competitive activities." This had
to be so, because no modern writer of the kind I am discussing—no one capable of using phrases like "objective consideration of contemporary phenomena"—would ever tabulate
his thoughts in that precise and detailed way. The whole tendency of modern prose is away from concreteness. Now analyse
these two sentences a little more closely. The first contains
forty-nine words but only sixty syllables, and all its words are
those of everyday life. The second contains thirty-eight words
of ninety syllables: eighteen of its words are from Latin roots,

and one from Greek. The first sentence contains six vivid images, and only one phrase ("time and chance") that could be called vague. The second contains not a single fresh, arresting phrase, and in spite of its ninety syllables it gives only a shortened version of the meaning contained in the first. Yet without a doubt it is the second kind of sentence that is gaining ground in modern English. I do not want to exaggerate. This kind of writing is not yet universal, and outcrops of simplicity will occur here and there in the worst-written page. Still, if you or I were told to write a few lines on the uncertainty of human fortunes, we should probably come much nearer to my imaginary sentence than to the one from *Ecclesiastes*.

As I have tried to show, modern writing at its worst does not consist in picking out words for the sake of their meaning and inventing images in order to make the meaning clearer. It consists in gumming together long strips of words which have already been set in order by someone else, and making the results presentable by sheer humbug. The attraction of this way of writing is that it is easy. It is easier—even quicker, once you have the habit—to say *In my opinion it is not an unjustifiable assumption that* than to say *I think*. If you use ready-made phrases, you not only don't have to hunt about for words; you also don't have to bother with the rhythms of your sentences, since these phrases are generally so arranged as to be more or less euphonious. When you are composing in a hurry—when you are dictating to a stenographer, for instance, or making a public speech—it is natural to fall into a pretentious, Latinized style. Tags like *a consideration which we should do well to bear in mind* or *a conclusion to which all of us would readily assent* will save many a sentence from coming down with a bump. By using stale metaphors, similes and idioms, you save much mental effort, at the cost of leaving your meaning vague, not only for your reader but for yourself. This is the significance of mixed metaphors. The sole aim of a metaphor is to call up a visual image. When these images clash—as in *The Fascist octopus has sung its swan song, the jackboot is thrown into the melting pot*—it can be taken as certain that the writer is not seeing a mental image of the objects he is naming; in other words he is not really thinking. Look again at the examples I gave at the beginning of this essay. Professor Laski (1) uses five negatives in fifty-three words. One of these is superfluous, making nonsense of the whole passage, and in addition there is the slip *alien* for akin, making further nonsense, and several avoidable pieces of clumsiness which increase the general vagueness. Professor Hogben (2) plays ducks and drakes with a battery which is able to write prescriptions, and, while disapproving of the everyday phrase *put up with,* is unwilling to look *egregious* up in the dictionary and see what it means; (3), if one takes an uncharitable attitude towards it, is simply meaningless: probably one could work out its intended meaning by reading the whole of the article in which it occurs. In (4), the writer knows more or less what he wants to say, but an accumulation of stale phrases chokes him like tea leaves blocking a sink. In (5), words and meaning have almost parted company. People who write in this manner usually have a general emotional meaning—they dislike one thing and want to express solidarity with another—but they are not interested in the detail of what they are saying. A scrupulous writer, in every sentence that he writes, will ask himself at least four questions, thus: What am I trying to say? What words will express it? What image or idiom will make it clearer? Is this image fresh enough to have an effect? And he will probably ask himself two more: Could I put it more shortly? Have I said anything that is avoidably ugly? But you are not obliged to go to all this trouble. You can shirk it by simply throwing your mind open and letting the ready-made phrases come crowding in. They will construct your sentences for you—even think your thoughts for you, to a certain extent—and at need they will perform the important service of partially concealing your meaning even from yourself. It is at this point that the special connection between politics and the debasement of language becomes clear.

In our time it is broadly true that political writing is bad writing. Where it is not true, it will generally be found that the writer is some kind of rebel, expressing his private opinions and not a "party line." Orthodoxy, of whatever color, seems to demand a lifeless, imitative style. The political dialects to be found in pamphlets, leading articles, manifestos, White Papers and the speeches of under-secretaries do, of course, vary from party to party, but they are all alike in that one almost never finds in them a fresh, vivid, home-made turn of speech. When one watches some tired hack on the platform mechanically repeating the familiar phrases—*bestial atrocities, iron heel, bloodstained tyranny, free peoples of the world, stand shoulder to shoulder*—one often has a curious feeling that one is not watching a live human being but some kind of dummy: a feeling which suddenly becomes stronger at moments when the light catches the speaker's spectacles and turns them into blank discs which seem to have no eyes behind them. And this is not altogether fanciful. A speaker who uses that kind of phraseology has gone some distance towards turning himself into a machine. The appropriate noises are coming out of his larynx, but his brain is not involved as it would be if he were choosing his words for himself. If the speech he is making is one that he is accustomed to make over and over again, he may be almost unconscious of what he is saying, as one is when one utters the responses in church. And this reduced state of consciousness, if not indispensable, is at any rate favorable to political conformity.

In our time, political speech and writing are largely the defence of the indefensible. Things like the continuance of British rule in India, the Russian purges and deportations, the dropping of the atom bombs on Japan, can indeed be defended, but only by arguments which are too brutal for most people to face, and which do not square with the professed aims of political parties. Thus political language has to consist largely of euphemism, question-begging and sheer cloudy vagueness. Defenceless villages are bombarded from the air, the inhabitants driven out into the countryside, the cattle machine-gunned, the huts set on fire with incendiary bullets: this is called *pacification*. Millions of peasants are robbed of their farms and sent trudging along the roads with no more than they can carry: this is called *transfer of population* or *rectification of frontiers*. People are imprisoned for years without trial, or shot in the back of the neck or sent to die of scurvy in Arctic lumber camps: this is called *elimination of unreliable elements*. Such phraseology is needed if one wants to name things without calling up mental pictures of them. Consider for instance some comfortable English professor defending Russian totalitarianism. He cannot say outright, "I believe in killing off your opponents when you can get good results by doing so." Probably, therefore, he will say something like this:

"While freely conceding that the Soviet régime exhibits certain features which the humanitarian may be inclined to deplore, we must, I think, agree that a certain curtailment of the right to political opposition is an unavoidable concomitant of transitional periods, and that the rigors which the Russian people have been called upon to undergo have been amply justified in the sphere of concrete achievement."

The inflated style is itself a kind of euphemism. A mass of Latin words falls upon the facts like soft snow, blurring the outlines and covering up all the details. The great enemy of clear language is insincerity. When there is a gap between one's real and one's declared aims, one turns as it were instinctively to long words and exhausted idioms, like a cuttlefish squirting out ink. In our age there is no such thing as "keeping out of politics." All issues are political issues, and politics itself is a mass of lies, evasions, folly, hatred and schizophrenia. When the general atmosphere is bad, language must suffer. I should expect to find—this is a guess which I have not sufficient knowledge to verify—that the German, Russian and Italian languages have all deteriorated in the last ten or fifteen years, as a result of dictatorship.

But if thought corrupts language, language can also corrupt thought. A bad usage can spread by tradition and imitation, even among people who should and do know better. The debased language that I have been discussing is in some ways very convenient. Phrases like *a not unjustifiable assumption, leaves much to be desired, would serve no good purpose, a consideration which we should do well to bear in mind,* are a continuous temptation, a packet of aspirins always at one's elbow. Look back through this essay, and for certain you will find that I have again and again committed the very faults I am protesting against. By this morning's post I have received a pamphlet dealing with conditions in Germany. The author tells me that he "felt impelled" to write it. I open it at random, and here is almost the first sentence that I see: "[The Allies] have an opportunity not only of achieving a radical transformation of Germany's social and political structure in such a way as to avoid a nationalistic reaction in Germany itself, but at the same time of laying the foundations of a co-operative and unified Europe." You see, he "feels impelled" to write—feels, presumably, that he has something new to say—and yet his words, like cavalry horses answering the bugle, group themselves automatically into the familiar dreary pattern. This invasion of one's mind by ready-made phrases (*lay the foundations, achieve a radical transformation*) can only be prevented if one is constantly on guard against them, and every such phrase anaesthetizes a portion of one's brain.

I said earlier that the decadence of our language is probably curable. Those who deny this would argue, if they produced an argument at all, that language merely reflects existing social conditions, and that we cannot influence its development by any direct tinkering with words and constructions. So far as the general tone or spirit of a language goes, this may be true, but it is not true in detail. Silly words and expressions have often disappeared, not through any evolutionary process but owing to the conscious action of a minority. Two recent examples were *explore every avenue* and *leave no stone unturned,* which were killed by the jeers of a few journalists. There is a long list of flyblown metaphors which could similarly be got rid of if enough people would interest themselves in the job; and it should also be possible to laugh the *not un-* formation out of existence,[1] to reduce the amount of Latin and Greek in the average sentence, to drive out foreign phrases and strayed scientific words, and, in general, to make pretentiousness unfashionable. But all these are minor points. The defence of the English language implies more than this, and perhaps it is best to start by saying what it does *not* imply.

To begin with it has nothing to do with archaism, with the salvaging of obsolete words and turns of speech, or with the setting up of a "standard English" which must never be departed from. On the contrary, it is especially concerned with the scrapping of every word or idiom which has outworn its usefulness. It has nothing to do with correct grammar and syntax, which are of no importance so long as one makes one's

[1] One can cure oneself of the *not un-* formation by memorizing this sentence: *A not unblack dog was chasing a not unsmall rabbit across a not ungreen field.*

meaning clear, or with the avoidance of Americanisms, or with having what is called a "good prose style." On the other hand it is not concerned with fake simplicity and the attempt to make written English colloquial. Nor does it even imply in every case preferring the Saxon word to the Latin one, though it does imply using the fewest and shortest words that will cover one's meaning. What is above all needed is to let the meaning choose the word, and not the other way about. In prose, the worst thing one can do with words is to surrender to them. When you think of a concrete object, you think wordlessly, and then, if you want to describe the thing you have been visualizing you probably hunt about till you find the exact words that seem to fit it. When you think of something abstract you are more inclined to use words from the start, and unless you make a conscious effort to prevent it, the existing dialect will come rushing in and do the job for you, at the expense of blurring or even changing your meaning. Probably it is better to put off using words as long as possible and get one's meaning as clear as one can through pictures or sensations. Afterwards one can choose—not simply *accept*—the phrases that will best cover the meaning, and then switch round and decide what impression one's words are likely to make on another person. This last effort of the mind cuts out all stale or mixed images, all prefabricated phrases, needless repetitions, and humbug and vagueness generally. But one can often be in doubt about the effect of a word or a phrase, and one needs rules that one can rely on when instinct fails. I think the following rules will cover most cases:

(i) Never use a metaphor, simile or other figure of speech which you are used to seeing in print.

(ii) Never use a long word where a short one will do.

(iii) If it is possible to cut a word out, always cut it out.

(iv) Never use the passive where you can use the active.

(v) Never use a foreign phrase, a scientific word or a jargon word if you can think of an everyday English equivalent.

(vi) Break any of these rules sooner than say anything outright barbarous.

These rules sound elementary, and so they are, but they demand a deep change of attitude in anyone who has grown used to writing in the style now fashionable. One could keep all of them and still write bad English, but one could not write the kind of stuff that I quoted in those five specimens at the beginning of this article.

I have not here been considering the literary use of language, but merely language as an instrument for expressing and not for concealing or preventing thought. Stuart Chase and others have come near to claiming that all abstract words are meaningless, and have used this as a pretext for advocating a kind of political quietism. Since you don't know what Fascism is, how can you struggle against Fascism? One need not swallow such absurdities as this, but one ought to recognize that the present political chaos is connected with the decay of language, and that one can probably bring about some improvement by starting at the verbal end. If you simplify your English, you are freed from the worst follies of orthodoxy. You cannot speak any of the necessary dialects, and when you make a stupid remark its stupidity will be obvious, even to yourself. Political language—and with variations this is true of all political parties, from Conservatives to Anarchists—is designed to make lies sound truthful and murder respectable, and to give an appearance of solidity to pure wind. One cannot change this all in a moment, but one can at least change one's own habits, and from time to time one can even, if one jeers loudly enough, send some worn-out and useless phrase—some *jackboot, Achilles' heel, hotbed, melting pot, acid test, veritable inferno* or other lump of verbal refuse—into the dustbin where it belongs.

Reflections on Gandhi

SAINTS SHOULD ALWAYS BE JUDGED GUILTY UNTIL THEY ARE proved innocent, but the tests that have to be applied to them are not, of course, the same in all cases. In Gandhi's case the questions one feels inclined to ask are: to what extent was Gandhi moved by vanity—by the consciousness of himself as a humble, naked old man, sitting on a praying mat and shaking empires by sheer spiritual power—and to what extent did he compromise his own principles by entering politics, which of their nature are inseparable from coercion and fraud? To give a definite answer one would have to study Gandhi's acts and writings in immense detail, for his whole life was a sort of pilgrimage in which every act was significant. But this partial autobiography,[1] which ends in the nineteen-twenties, is strong evidence in his favor, all the more because it covers what he would have called the unregenerate part of his life and reminds one that inside the saint, or near-saint, there was a very shrewd, able person who could, if he had chosen, have been a brilliant success as a lawyer, an administrator or perhaps even a businessman.

At about the time when the autobiography first appeared I remember reading its opening chapters in the ill-printed pages of some Indian newspaper. They made a good impression on me, which Gandhi himself at that time, did not. The

[1] *The Story of my Experiments with Truth.* By M. K. Gandhi. Translated from the Gujarati by Mahadex Desai. Public Affairs Press.

things that one associated with him—home-spun cloth, "soul forces" and vegetarianism—were unappealing, and his medievalist program was obviously not viable in a backward, starving, over-populated country. It was also apparent that the British were making use of him, or thought they were making use of him. Strictly speaking, as a Nationalist, he was an enemy, but since in every crisis he would exert himself to prevent violence—which, from the British point of view, meant preventing any effective action whatever—he could be regarded as "our man." In private this was sometimes cynically admitted. The attitude of the Indian millionaires was similar. Gandhi called upon them to repent, and naturally they preferred him to the Socialists and Communists who, given the chance, would actually have taken their money away. How reliable such calculations are in the long run is doubtful; as Gandhi himself says, "in the end deceivers deceive only themselves"; but at any rate the gentleness with which he was nearly always handled was due partly to the feeling that he was useful. The British Conservatives only became really angry with him when, as in 1942, he was in effect turning his non-violence against a different conqueror.

But I could see even then that the British officials who spoke of him with a mixture of amusement and disapproval also genuinely liked and admired him, after a fashion. Nobody ever suggested that he was corrupt, or ambitious in any vulgar way, or that anything he did was actuated by fear or malice. In judging a man like Gandhi one seems instinctively to apply high standards, so that some of his virtues have passed almost unnoticed. For instance, it is clear even from the autobiography that his natural physical courage was quite outstanding: the manner of his death was a later illustration of this, for a public man who attached any value to his own skin would have been more adequately guarded. Again, he seems to have been quite free from that maniacal suspiciousness which, as E. M. Forster rightly says in *A Passage to India,* is the besetting Indian vice, as hypocrisy is the British vice. Although no doubt he was shrewd enough in detecting dishonesty, he seems wherever possible to have believed that other people were acting in good faith and had a better nature through which they could be approached. And though he came of a poor middle-class family, started life rather unfavorably, and was probably of unimpressive physical appearance, he was not afflicted by envy or by the feeling of inferiority. Color feeling when he first met it in its worst form in South Africa, seems rather to have astonished him. Even when he was fighting what was in effect a color war, he did not think of people in terms of race or status. The governor of a province, a cotton millionaire, a half-starved Dravidian coolie, a British private soldier were all equally human beings, to be approached in much the same way. It is noticeable that even in the worst possible circumstances, as in South Africa when he was making himself unpopular as the champion of the Indian community, he did not lack European friends.

Written in short lengths for newspaper serialization, the autobiography is not a literary masterpiece, but it is the more impressive because of the commonplaceness of much of its material. It is well to be reminded that Gandhi started out with the normal ambitions of a young Indian student and only adopted his extremist opinions by degrees and, in some cases, rather unwillingly. There was a time, it is interesting to learn, when he wore a top hat, took dancing lessons, studied French and Latin, went up the Eiffel Tower and even tried to learn the violin—all this was the idea of assimilating European civilization as thoroughly as possible. He was not one of those saints who are marked out by their phenomenal piety

from childhood onwards, nor one of the other kind who for-
sake the world after sensational debaucheries. He makes full
confession of the misdeeds of his youth, but in fact there is
not much to confess. As a frontispiece to the book there is a
photograph of Gandhi's possessions at the time of his death.
The whole outfit could be purchased for about £5, and
Gandhi's sins, at least his fleshly sins, would make the same
sort of appearance if placed all in one heap. A few cigarettes,
a few mouthfuls of meat, a few annas pilfered in childhood
from the maidservant, two visits to a brothel (on each occasion
he got away without "doing anything"), one narrowly escaped
lapse with his landlady in Plymouth, one outburst of temper—
that is about the whole collection. Almost from childhood
onwards he had a deep earnestness, an attitude ethical rather
than religious, but, until he was about thirty, no very definite
sense of direction. His first entry into anything describable as
public life was made by way of vegetarianism. Underneath his
less ordinary qualities one feels all the time the solid middle-
class businessmen who were his ancestors. One feels that even
after he had abandoned personal ambition he must have been
a resourceful, energetic lawyer and a hard-headed political or-
ganizer, careful in keeping down expenses, an adroit handler
of committees and an indefatigable chaser of subscriptions.
His character was an extraordinarily mixed one, but there
was almost nothing in it that you can put your finger on and
call bad, and I believe that even Gandhi's worst enemies
would admit that he was an interesting and unusual man
who enriched the world simply by being alive. Whether he was
also a lovable man, and whether his teachings can have much
value for those who do not accept the religious beliefs on
which they are founded, I have never felt fully certain.

Of late years it has been the fashion to talk about Gandhi as though he were not only sympathetic to the Western Left-wing movement, but were integrally part of it. Anarchists and pacifists, in particular, have claimed him for their own, noticing only that he was opposed to centralism and State violence and ignoring the other-worldly, anti-humanist tendency of his doctrines. But one should, I think, realize that Gandhi's teachings cannot be squared with the belief that Man is the measure of all things and that our job is to make life worth living on this earth, which is the only earth we have. They make sense only on the assumption that God exists and that the world of solid objects is an illusion to be escaped from. It is worth considering the disciplines which Gandhi imposed on himself and which—though he might not insist on every one of his followers observing every detail—he considered indispensable if one wanted to serve either God or humanity. First of all, no meat-eating, and if possible no animal food in any form. (Gandhi himself, for the sake of his health, had to compromise on milk, but seems to have felt this to be a backsliding.) No alcohol or tobacco, and no spices or condiments even of a vegetable kind, since food should be taken not for its own sake but solely in order to preserve one's strength. Secondly, if possible, no sexual intercourse. If sexual intercourse must happen, then it should be for the sole purpose of begetting children and presumably at long intervals. Gandhi himself, in his middle thirties, took the vow of *brahmacharya*, which means not only complete chastity but the elimination of sexual desire. This condition, it seems, is difficult to attain without a special diet and frequent fasting. One of the dangers of milk-drinking is that it is apt to arouse sexual desire. And finally—this is the cardinal point—for the seeker after goodness there must be no close friendships and no exclusive loves whatever.

Close friendships, Gandhi says, are dangerous, because "friends react on one another" and through loyalty to a friend one can be led into wrong-doing. This is unquestionably true. Moreover, if one is to love God, or to love humanity as a whole, one cannot give one's preference to any individual person. This again is true, and it marks the point at which the humanistic and the religious attitude cease to be reconcilable. To an ordinary human being, love means nothing if it does not mean loving some people more than others. The autobiography leaves it uncertain whether Gandhi behaved in an inconsiderate way to his wife and children, but at any rate it makes clear that on three occasions he was willing to let his wife or a child die rather than administer the animal food prescribed by the doctor. It is true that the threatened death never actually occurred, and also that Gandhi—with, one gathers, a good deal of moral pressure in the opposite direction—always gave the patient the choice of staying alive at the price of committing a sin: still, if the decision had been solely his own, he would have forbidden the animal food, whatever the risks might be. There must, he says, be some limit to what we will do in order to remain alive, and the limit is well on this side of chicken broth. This attitude is perhaps a noble one, but, in the sense which—I think—most people would give to the word, it is inhuman. The essence of being human is that one does not seek perfection, that one *is* sometimes willing to commit sins for the sake of loyalty, that one does not push asceticism to the point where it makes friendly intercourse impossible, and that one is prepared in the end to be defeated and broken up by life, which is the inevitable price of fastening one's love upon other human individuals. No doubt alcohol, tobacco, and so forth, are things that a saint must avoid, but sainthood is also a thing that human beings must avoid. There is an obvious retort to this, but one should be wary about making it. In this yogi-ridden age, it is too readily assumed that "non-attachment" is not only better than a full acceptance of earthly life, but that the ordinary man only rejects it because it is too difficult: in other words, that the average human being is a failed saint. It is doubtful whether this is true. Many people genuinely do not wish to be saints, and it is probable that some who achieve or aspire to sainthood have never felt much temptation to be human beings. If one could follow it to its psychological roots, one would, I believe, find that the main motive for "non-attachment" is a desire to escape from the pain of living, and above all from love, which, sexual or non-sexual, is hard work. But it is not necessary here to argue whether the other-worldly or the humanistic ideal is "higher." The point is that they are incompatible. One must choose between God and Man, and all "radicals" and "progressives," from the mildest Liberal to the most extreme Anarchist, have in effect chosen Man.

However, Gandhi's pacifism can be separated to some extent from his other teachings. Its motive was religious, but he claimed also for it that it was a definite technique, a method, capable of producing desired political results. Gandhi's attitude was not that of most Western pacifists. *Satyagraha,* first evolved in South Africa, was a sort of non-violent warfare, a way of defeating the enemy without hurting him and without feeling or arousing hatred. It entailed such things as civil disobedience, strikes, lying down in front of railway trains, enduring police charges without running away and without hitting back, and the like. Gandhi objected to "passive resistance" as a translation of *Satyagraha:* in Gujarati, it seems, the word means "firmness in the truth." In his early days Gandhi served as a stretcher-bearer on the British side in the Boer War, and he was prepared to do the

same again in the war of 1914-18. Even after he had completely abjured violence he was honest enough to see that in
war it is usually necessary to take sides. He did not—indeed,
since his whole political life centred round a struggle for
national independence, he could not—take the sterile and
dishonest line of pretending that in every war both sides are
exactly the same and it makes no difference who wins. Nor
did he, like most Western pacifists, specialize in avoiding
awkward questions. In relation to the late war, one question
that every pacifist had a clear obligation to answer was:
"What about the Jews? Are you prepared to see them exter-
minated? If not, how do you propose to save them without
resorting to war?" I must say that I have never heard, from
any Western pacifist, an honest answer to this question,
though I have heard plenty of evasions, usually of the "you're
another" type. But it so happens that Gandhi was asked a
somewhat similar question in 1938 and that his answer is on
record in Mr. Louis Fischer's *Gandhi and Stalin.* According to
Mr. Fischer, Gandhi's view was that the German Jews ought
to commit collective suicide, which "would have aroused the
world and the people of Germany to Hitler's violence." After
the war he justified himself: the Jews had been killed any-
way, and might as well have died significantly. One has the
impression that this attitude staggered even so warm an admirer as Mr. Fischer, but Gandhi was merely being honest. If
you are not prepared to take life, you must often be prepared
for lives to be lost in some other way. When, in 1942, he
urged non-violent resistance against a Japanese invasion, he
was ready to admit that it might cost several million deaths.

At the same time there is reason to think that Gandhi,
who after all was born in 1869, did not understand the nature of totalitarianism and saw everything in terms of his own
struggle against the British government. The important point

here is not so much that the British treated him forbearingly
as that he was always able to command publicity. As can be
seen from the phrase quoted above, he believed in "arousing
the world," which is only possible if the world gets a chance
to hear what you are doing. It is difficult to see how Gandhi's
methods could be applied in a country where opponents of
the régime disappear in the middle of the night and are never
heard of again. Without a free Press and the right of assembly,
it is impossible not merely to appeal to outside opinion, but
to bring a mass movement into being, or even to make your
intentions known to your adversary. Is there a Gandhi in
Russia at this moment? And if there is, what is he accomplish-
ing? The Russian masses could only practice civil disobedience if the same idea happened to occur to all of them simultaneously, and even then, to judge by the history of the
Ukraine famine, it would make no difference. But let it be
granted that non-violent resistance can be effective against
one's own government, or against an occupying power: even
so, how does one put it into practice internationally? Gandhi's
various conflicting statements on the late war seem to show
that he felt the difficulty of this. Applied to foreign politics,
pacifism either stops being pacifist or becomes appeasement.
Moreover the assumption, which served Gandhi so well in
dealing with individuals, that all human beings are more or
less approachable and will respond to a generous gesture,
needs to be seriously questioned. It is not necessarily true, for
example, when you are dealing with lunatics. Then the question becomes: Who is sane? Was Hitler sane? And is it not
possible for one whole culture to be insane by the standards
of another? And, so far as one can gauge the feelings of whole
nations, is there any apparent connection between a generous
deed and a friendly response? Is gratitude a factor in international politics?

These and kindred questions need discussion, and need it urgently, in the few years left to us before somebody presses the button and the rockets begin to fly. It seems doubtful whether civilization can stand another major war, and it is at least thinkable that the way out lies through non-violence. It is Gandhi's virtue that he would have been ready to give honest consideration to the kind of question that I have raised above; and, indeed, he probably did discuss most of these questions somewhere or other in his innumerable newspaper articles. One feels of him that there was much that he did not understand, but not that there was anything that he was frightened of saying or thinking. I have never been able to feel much liking for Gandhi, but I do not feel sure that as a political thinker he was wrong in the main, nor do I believe that his life was a failure. It is curious that when he was assassinated, many of his warmest admirers exclaimed sorrowfully that he had lived just long enough to see his life work in ruins, because India was engaged in a civil war which had always been foreseen as one of the by-products of the transfer of power. But it was not in trying to smooth down Hindu-Moslem rivalry that Gandhi had spent his life. His main political objective, the peaceful ending of British rule, had after all been attained. As usual the relevant facts cut across one another. On the other hand, the British did get out of India without fighting, an event which very few observers indeed would have predicted until about a year before it happened. On the other hand, this was done by a Labour government, and it is certain that a Conservative government, especially a government headed by Churchill, would have acted differently. But if, by 1945, there had grown up in Britain a large body of opinion sympathetic to Indian independence, how far was this due to Gandhi's personal influence? And if, as may happen, India and Britain finally settle down into a decent and friendly relationship, will this be partly because Gandhi, by keeping up his struggle obstinately and without hatred, disinfected the political air? That one even thinks of asking such questions indicates his stature. One may feel, as I do, a sort of aesthetic distaste for Gandhi, one may reject the claims of sainthood made on his behalf (he never made any such claim himself, by the way), one may also reject sainthood as an ideal and therefore feel that Gandhi's basic aims were anti-human and reactionary: but regarded simply as a politician, and compared with the other leading political figures of our time, how clean a smell he has managed to leave behind!

The Prevention of Literature

ABOUT A YEAR AGO I ATTENDED A MEETING OF THE P.E.N. CLUB,
the occasion being the tercentenary of Milton's *Areopagitica*—
a pamphlet, it may be remembered, in defence of freedom of
the Press. Milton's famous phrase about the sin of "killing"
a book was printed on the leaflets advertising the meeting
which had been circulated beforehand.

There were four speakers on the platform. One of them
delivered a speech which did deal with the freedom of the
Press, but only in relation to India; another said, hesitantly,
and in very general terms, that liberty was a good thing; a
third delivered an attack on the laws relating to obscenity in
literature. The fourth devoted most of his speech to a defence
of the Russian purges. Of the speeches from the body of the
hall, some reverted to the question of obscenity and the laws
that deal with it, others were simply eulogies of Soviet Russia.
Moral liberty—the liberty to discuss sex questions frankly in
print—seemed to be generally approved, but political liberty
was not mentioned. Out of this concourse of several hundred
people, perhaps half of whom were directly connected with
the writing trade, there was not a single one who could point
out that freedom of the Press, if it means anything at all,
means the freedom to criticize and oppose. Significantly, no
speaker quoted from the pamphlet which was ostensibly being
commemorated. Nor was there any mention of the various

books that have been "killed" in England and the United States during the war. In its net effect the meeting was a demonstration in favor of censorship.[1]

There was nothing particularly surprising in this. In our age, the idea of intellectual liberty is under attack from two directions. On the one side are its theoretical enemies, the apologists of totalitarianism, and on the other its immediate, practical enemies, monopoly and bureaucracy. Any writer or journalist who wants to retain his integrity finds himself thwarted by the general drift of society rather than by active persecution. The sort of things that are working against him are the concentration of the Press in the hands of a few rich men, the grip of monopoly on radio and the films, the unwillingness of the public to spend money on books, making it necessary for nearly every writer to earn part of his living by hackwork, the encroachment of official bodies like the M.O.I. and the British Council, which help the writer to keep alive but also waste his time and dictate his opinions, and the continuous war atmosphere of the past ten years, whose distorting effects no one has been able to escape. Everything in our age conspires to turn the writer, and every other kind of artist as well, into a minor official, working on themes handed down from above and never telling what seems to him the whole of the truth. But in struggling against this fate he gets no help from his own side: that is, there is no large body of opinion which will assure him that he is in the right. In the past, at any rate throughout the Protestant centuries, the idea of re-

[1] It is fair to say that the P.E.N. Club celebrations, which lasted a week or more, did not always stick at quite the same level. I happened to strike a bad day. But an examination of the speeches (printed under the title *Freedom of Expression*) shows that almost nobody in our own day is able to speak out as roundly in favor of intellectual liberty as Milton could do 300 years ago—and this in spite of the fact Milton was writing in a period of civil war.

bellion and the idea of intellectual integrity were mixed up.
A heretic—political, moral, religious, or aesthetic—was one who
refused to outrage his own conscience. His outlook was
summed up in the words of the Revivalist hymn:

> Dare to be a Daniel,
> Dare to stand alone;
> Dare to have a purpose firm,
> Dare to make it known.

To bring this hymn up to date one would have to add a
"Don't" at the beginning of each line. For it is the peculiarity
of our age that the rebels against the existing order, at any
rate the most numerous and characteristic of them, are also
rebelling against the idea of individual integrity. "Daring to
stand alone" is ideologically criminal as well as practically
dangerous. The independence of the writer and the artist is
eaten away by vague economic forces, and at the same time it
is undermined by those who should be its defenders. It is with
the second process that I am concerned here.

Freedom of thought and of the Press are usually attacked
by arguments which are not worth bothering about. Anyone
who has experience of lecturing and debating knows them off
backwards. Here I am not trying to deal with the familiar
claim that freedom is an illusion, or with the claim that there
is more freedom in totalitarian countries than in democratic
ones, but with the much more tenable and dangerous proposi-
tion that freedom is *undesirable* and that intellectual honesty
is a form of anti-social selfishness. Although other aspects of
the question are usually in the foreground, the controversy
over freedom of speech and of the Press is at bottom a controversy over the desirability, or otherwise, of telling lies. What
is really at issue is the right to report contemporary events
truthfully, or as truthfully as is consistent with the ignorance,

bias and self-deception from which every observer necessarily suffers. In saying this I may seem to be saying that straightforward "reportage" is the only branch of literature that matters: but I will try to show later that at every literary level, and probably in every one of the arts, the same issue arises in more or less subtilized forms. Meanwhile, it is necessary to strip away the irrelevancies in which this controversy is usually wrapped up.

The enemies of intellectual liberty always try to present their case as a plea for discipline versus individualism. The issue truth-versus-untruth is as far as possible kept in the background. Although the point of emphasis may vary, the writer who refuses to sell his opinions is always branded as a mere *egoist*. He is accused, that is, either of wanting to shut himself up in an ivory tower, or of making an exhibitionist display of his own personality, or of resisting the inevitable current of history in an attempt to cling to unjustified privileges. The Catholic and the Communist are alike in assuming that an opponent cannot be both honest and intelligent. Each of them tacitly claims that "the truth" has already been revealed, and that the heretic, if he is not simply a fool, is secretly aware of "the truth" and merely resists it out of selfish motives. In Communist literature the attack on intellectual liberty is usually masked by oratory about "petty-bourgeois individualism," "the illusions of nineteenth-century liberalism," etc., and backed up by words of abuse such as "romantic" and "sentimental," which, since they do not have any agreed meaning, are difficult to answer. In this way the controversy is maneuvered away from its real issue. One can accept, and most enlightened people would accept, the Communist thesis that pure freedom will only exist in a classless society, and that one is most nearly free when one is working to bring such a society about. But slipped in with this is the quite unfounded claim that the Communist party is itself aiming at the establishment of the classless society, and that in the U.S.S.R. this aim is actually on the way to being realized. If the first claim is allowed to entail the second, there is almost no assault on common sense and common decency that cannot be justified. But meanwhile, the real point has been dodged. Freedom of the intellect means the freedom to report what one has seen, heard, and felt, and not to be obliged to fabricate imaginary facts and feelings. The familiar tirades against "escapism," and "individualism," "romanticism" and so forth, are merely a forensic device, the aim of which is to make the perversion of history seem respectable.

Fifteen years ago, when one defended the freedom of the intellect, one had to defend it against Conservatives, against Catholics, and to some extent—for they were not of great importance in England—against Fascists. Today one has to defend it against Communists and "fellow-travellers." One ought not to exaggerate the direct influence of the small English Communist party, but there can be no question about the poisonous effect of the Russian *mythos* on English intellectual life. Because of it known facts are suppressed and distorted to such an extent as to make it doubtful whether a true history of our times can ever be written. Let me give just one instance out of the hundreds that could be cited. When Germany collapsed, it was found that very large numbers of Soviet Russians—mostly, no doubt, from non-political motives—had changed sides and were fighting for the Germans. Also, a small but not negligible proportion of the Russian prisoners and Displaced Persons refused to go back to the U.S.S.R., and some of them, at least, were repatriated against their will. These facts, known to many journalists on the spot, went almost unmentioned in the British Press, while at the same time Russophile publicists in England continued to justify the purges and deportations of 1936-38 by claiming that the U.S.S.R. "had no quislings." The fog of lies and misinformation that surrounds such subjects as the Ukraine famine, the Spanish civil war, Russian policy in Poland, and so forth, is not due entirely to conscious dishonesty, but any writer or journalist who is fully sympathetic to the U.S.S.R.—sympathetic, that is, in the way the Russians themselves would want him to be— does have to acquiesce in deliberate falsification on important issues. I have before me what must be a very rare pamphlet, written by Maxim Litvinoff in 1918 and outlining the recent events in the Russian Revolution. It makes no mention of Stalin, but gives high praise to Trotsky, and also to Zinoviev, Kamenev, and others. What could be the attitude of even the most intellectually scrupulous Communist towards such a pamphlet? At best, the obscurantist attitude of saying that it is an undesirable document and better suppressed. And if for some reason it were decided to issue a garbled version of the pamphlet, denigrating Trotsky and inserting references to Stalin, no Communist who remained faithful to his party could protest. Forgeries almost as gross as this have been committed in recent years. But the significant thing is not that they happen, but that, even when they are known about, they provoke no reaction from the Left-wing intelligentsia as a whole. The argument that to tell the truth would be "inopportune" or would "play into the hands of" somebody or other is felt to be unanswerable, and few people are bothered by the prospect of the lies which they condone getting out of the newspapers and into the history books.

The organized lying practised by totalitarian states is not, as is sometimes claimed, a temporary expedient of the same nature as military deception. It is something integral to totalitarianism, something that would still continue even if concentration camps and secret police forces had ceased to be

necessary. Among intelligent Communists there is an underground legend to the effect that although the Russian government is obliged *now* to deal in lying propaganda, frame-up
trials, and so forth, it is secretly recording the true facts and
will publish them at some future time. We can, I believe, be
quite certain that this is not the case, because the mentality
implied by such an action is that of a liberal historian who
believes that the past cannot be altered and that a correct
knowledge of history is valuable as a matter of course. From
the totalitarian point of view history is something to be
created rather than learned. A totalitarian state is in effect a
theocracy, and its ruling caste, in order to keep its position, has
to be thought of as infallible. But since, in practice, no one
is infallible, it is frequently necessary to rearrange past events
in order to show that this or that mistake was not made, or
that this or that imaginary triumph actually happened. Then,
again, every major change in policy demands a corresponding
change of doctrine and a revaluation of prominent historical
figures. This kind of thing happens everywhere, but is clearly
likelier to lead to outright falsification in societies where only
one opinion is permissible at any given moment. Totalitarianism demands, in fact, the continuous alteration of the past,
and in the long run probably demands a disbelief in the very
existence of objective truth. The friends of totalitarianism
in this country usually tend to argue that since absolute
truth is not attainable, a big lie is no worse than a little lie.
It is pointed out that *all* historical records are biased and
inaccurate, or, on the other hand, that modern physics has
proved that what seems to us the real world is an illusion, so
that to believe in the evidence of one's senses is simply vulgar
philistinism. A totalitarian society which succeeded in per-
petuating itself would probably set up a schizophrenic system
of thought, in which the laws of common sense held good in

everyday life and in certain exact sciences, but could be disregarded by the politician, the historian, and the sociologist. Already there are countless people who would think it scandalous to falsify a scientific textbook, but would see nothing wrong in falsifying an historical fact. It is at the point where literature and politics cross that totalitarianism exerts its greatest pressure on the intellectual. The exact sciences are not, at this date, menaced to anything like the same extent. This partly accounts for the fact that in all countries it is easier for the scientists than for the writers to line up behind their respective governments.

To keep the matter in perspective, let me repeat what I said at the beginning of this essay: that in England the *immediate* enemies of truthfulness, and hence of freedom of thought, are the Press lords, the film magnates, and the bureaucrats, but that on a long view the weakening of the desire for liberty among the intellectuals themselves is the most serious symptom of all. It may seem that all this time I have been talking about the effects of censorship, not on literature as a whole, but merely on one department of political journalism. Granted that Soviet Russia constitutes a sort of forbidden area in the British Press, granted that issues like Poland, the Spanish civil war, the Russo-German pact, and so forth, are debarred from serious discussion, and that if you possess information that conflicts with the prevailing orthodoxy you are expected either to distort it or keep quiet about it—granted all this, why should literature in the wider sense be affected? Is every writer a politician, and is every book necessarily a work of straightforward "reportage"? Even under the tightest dictatorship, cannot the individual writer remain free inside his own mind and distil or disguise his unorthodox ideas in such a way that the authorities will be too stupid to recognize them? And in any case, if the writer himself is in agreement with the prevailing orthodoxy, why should it have a cramping effect on him? Is not literature, or any of the arts, likeliest to flourish in societies in which there are no major conflicts of opinion and no sharp distinction between the artist and his audience? Does one have to assume that every writer is a rebel, or even that a writer as such is an exceptional person?

Whenever one attempts to defend intellectual liberty against the claims of totalitarianism, one meets with these arguments in one form or another. They are based on a complete misunderstanding of what literature is, and how—one should perhaps rather say *why*—it comes into being. They assume that a writer is either a mere entertainer or else a venal hack who can switch from one line of propaganda to another as easily as an organ grinder changing tunes. But after all, how is it that books ever come to be written? Above a quite low level, literature is an attempt to influence the viewpoint of one's contemporaries by recording experience. And so far as freedom of expression is concerned, there is not much difference between a mere journalist and the most "unpolitical" imaginative writer. The journalist is unfree, and is conscious of unfreedom, when he is forced to write lies or suppress what seems to him important news: the imaginative writer is unfree when he has to falsify his subjective feelings, which from his point of view are facts. He may distort and caricature reality in order to make his meaning clearer, but he cannot misrepresent the scenery of his own mind: he cannot say with any conviction that he likes what he dislikes, or believes what he disbelieves. If he is forced to do so, the only result is that his creative faculties dry up. Nor can he solve the problem by keeping away from controversial topics. There is no such thing as genuinely non-political literature, and least of all in an age like our own, when fears, hatreds, and loyalties of a directly political kind are near to the surface of everyone's consciousness. Even a single taboo can have an all-round crippling effect upon the mind, because there is always the danger that any thought which is freely followed up may lead to the forbidden thought. It follows that the atmosphere of totalitarianism is deadly to any kind of prose writer, though a poet, at any rate a lyric poet, might possibly find it breathable. And in any totalitarian society that survives for more than a couple of generations, it is probable that prose literature, of the kind that has existed during the past four hundred years, must actually *come to an end.*

Literature has sometimes flourished under despotic régimes, but, as has often been pointed out, the despotisms of the past were not totalitarian. Their repressive apparatus was always inefficient, their ruling classes were usually either corrupt or apathetic or half-liberal in outlook, and the prevailing religious doctrines usually worked against perfectionism and the notion of human infallibility. Even so it is broadly true that prose literature has reached its highest levels in periods of democracy and free speculation. What is new in totalitarianism is that its doctrines are not only unchallengeable but also unstable. They have to be accepted on pain of damnation, but on the other hand they are always liable to be altered at a moment's notice. Consider, for example, the various attitudes, completely incompatible with one another, which an English Communist or "fellow-traveller" has had to adopt towards the war between Britain and Germany. For years before September, 1939, he was expected to be in a continuous stew about "the horrors of Nazism" and to twist everything he wrote into a denunciation of Hitler: after September, 1939, for twenty months, he had to believe that Germany was more sinned against than sinning, and the word "Nazi," at least as far as print went, had to drop right out of his vocabulary. Immediately after hearing the 8 o'clock news bulletin on the morning of 22nd June, 1941, he had to start believing once again that Nazism was the most hideous evil the world had ever seen. Now, it is easy for a politician to make such changes: for a writer the case is somewhat different. If he is to switch his allegiance at exactly the right moment, he must either tell lies about his subjective feelings, or else suppress them altogether. In either case he has destroyed his dynamo. Not only will ideas refuse to come to him, but the very words he uses will seem to stiffen under his touch. Political writing in our time consists almost entirely of prefabricated phrases bolted together like the pieces of a child's Meccano set. It is the unavoidable result of self-censorship. To write in plain, vigorous language one has to think fearlessly, and if one thinks fearlessly one cannot be politically orthodox. It might be otherwise in an "age of faith," when the prevailing orthodoxy has been long established and is not taken too seriously. In that case it would be possible, or might be possible, for large areas of one's mind to remain unaffected by what one officially believed. Even so, it is worth noticing that prose literature almost disappeared during the only age of faith that Europe has ever enjoyed. Throughout the whole of the Middle Ages there was almost no imaginative prose literature and very little in the way of historical writing: and the intellectual leaders of society expressed their most serious thoughts in a dead language which barely altered during a thousand years.

Totalitarianism, however, does not so much promise an age of faith as an age of schizophrenia. A society becomes totalitarian when its structure becomes flagrantly artificial: that is, when its ruling class has lost its function but succeeds in clinging to power by force or fraud. Such a society, no matter how long it persists, can never afford to become either tolerant or intellectually stable. It can never permit either the truthful recording of facts, or the emotional sincerity, that literary creation demands. But to be corrupted by totalitarianism one does not have to live in a totalitarian country. The mere prevalence of certain ideas can spread a kind of poison that makes one subject after another impossible for literary purposes. Where-ever there is an enforced orthodoxy—or even two orthodoxies, as often happens—good writing stops. This was well illustrated by the Spanish civil war. To many English intellectuals the war was a deeply moving experience, but not an experience about which they could write sincerely. There were only two things that you were allowed to say, and both of them were palpable lies: as a result, the war produced acres of print but almost nothing worth reading.

It is not certain whether the effects of totalitarianism upon verse need be so deadly as its effects on prose. There is a whole series of converging reasons why it is somewhat easier for a poet than for a prose writer to feel at home in an authoritarian society. To begin with, bureaucrats and other "practical" men usually despise the poet too deeply to be much interested in what he is saying. Secondly, what the poet is saying—that is, what his poem "means" if translated into prose—is relatively unimportant even to himself. The thought contained in a poem is always simple, and is no more the primary purpose of the poem than the anecdote is the primary purpose of the pic-ture. A poem is an arrangement of sounds and associations, as a painting is an arrangement of brushmarks. For short snatches, indeed, as in the refrain of a song, poetry can even dispense with meaning altogether. It is therefore fairly easy for a poet to keep away from dangerous subjects and avoid utter-ing heresies: and even when he does utter them, they may escape notice. But above all, good verse, unlike good prose, is not necessarily an individual product. Certain kinds of poems, such as ballads, or, on the other hand, very artificial verse forms, can be composed co-operatively by groups of people.

Whether the ancient English and Scottish ballads were originally produced by individuals, or by the people at large, is disputed; but at any rate they are non-individual in the sense that they constantly change in passing from mouth to mouth. Even in print no two versions of a ballad are ever quite the same. Many primitive peoples compose verse communally. Someone begins to improvise, probably accompanying himself on a musical instrument, somebody else chips in with a line or a rhyme when the first singer breaks down, and so the process continues until there exists a whole song or ballad which has no identifiable author.

In prose, this kind of intimate collaboration is quite impossible. Serious prose, in any case, has to be composed in solitude, whereas the excitement of being part of a group is actually an aid to certain kinds of versification. Verse—and perhaps good verse of its kind, though it would not be the highest kind—might survive under even the most inquisitorial régime. Even in a society where liberty and individuality had been extinguished, there would still be need either for patriotic songs and heroic ballads celebrating victories, or for elaborate exercises in flattery: and these are the kinds of poem that can be written to order, or composed communally, without necessarily lacking artistic value. Prose is a different matter, since the prose writer cannot narrow the range of his thoughts without killing his inventiveness. But the history of totalitarian societies, or of groups of people who have adopted the totalitarian outlook, suggests that loss of liberty is inimical to *all* forms of literature. German literature almost disappeared during the Hitler régime, and the case was not much better in Italy. Russian literature, so far as one can judge by translations, has deteriorated markedly since the early days of the Revolution, though some of the verse appears to be better than the prose. Few if any Russian novels that it is possible to take seriously have been translated for about fifteen years. In western Europe and America large sections of the literary intelligentsia have either passed through the Communist party or have been warmly sympathetic to it, but this whole leftward movement has produced extraordinarily few books worth reading. Orthodox Catholicism, again, seems to have a crushing effect upon certain literary forms, especially the novel. During a period of three hundred years, how many people have been at once good novelists and good Catholics? The fact is that certain themes cannot be celebrated in words, and tyranny is one of them. No one ever wrote a good book in praise of the Inquisition. Poetry *might* survive in a totalitarian age, and certain arts or half-arts, such as architecture, might even find tyranny beneficial, but the prose writer would have no choice between silence and death. Prose literature as we know it is the product of rationalism, of the Protestant centuries, of the autonomous individual. And the destruction of intellectual liberty cripples the journalist, the sociological writer, the historian, the novelist, the critic, and the poet, in that order. In the future it is possible that a new kind of literature, not involving individual feeling or truthful observation, may arise, but no such thing is at present imaginable. It seems much likelier that if the liberal culture that we have lived in since the Renaissance actually comes to an end, the literary art will perish with it.

Of course, print will continue to be used, and it is interesting to speculate what kinds of reading matter would survive in a rigidly totalitarian society. Newspapers will presumably continue until television technique reaches a higher level, but apart from newspapers it is doubtful even now whether the great mass of people in the industrialized countries feel the need for any kind of literature. They are unwilling, at any rate, to spend anywhere near as much on reading matter as they spend on several other recreations. Probably novels and stories will be completely superseded by film and radio productions. Or perhaps some kind of low-grade sensational fiction will survive, produced by a sort of conveyor-belt process that reduces human initiative to the minimum.

It would probably not be beyond human ingenuity to write books by machinery. But a sort of mechanizing process can already be seen at work in the film and radio, in publicity and propaganda, and in the lower reaches of journalism. The Disney films, for instance, are produced by what is essentially a factory process, the work being done partly mechanically and partly by teams of artists who have to subordinate their individual style. Radio features are commonly written by tired hacks to whom the subject and the manner of treatment are dictated beforehand: even so, what they write is merely a kind of raw material to be chopped into shape by producers and censors. So also with the innumerable books and pamphlets commissioned by government departments. Even more machine-like is the production of short stories, serials, and poems for the very cheap magazines. Papers such as the *Writer* abound with advertisements of literary schools, all of them offering you ready-made plots at a few shillings a time. Some, together with the plot, supply the opening and closing sentences of each chapter. Others furnish you with a sort of algebraical formula by the use of which you can construct your plots for yourself. Others offer packs of cards marked with characters and situations, which have only to be shuffled and dealt in order to produce ingenious stories automatically. It is probably in some such way that the literature of a totalitarian society would be produced, if literature were still felt to be necessary. Imagination—even consciousness, so far as possible—would be eliminated from the process of writing. Books would be planned in their broad lines by bureaucrats, and would pass through so many hands that when finished they would be no more an individual product than a Ford car at the end of the assembly line. It goes without saying that anything so produced would be rubbish; but anything that was *not* rubbish would endanger the structure of the state. As for the surviving literature of the past, it would have to be suppressed or at least elaborately rewritten.

Meanwhile totalitarianism has not fully triumphed anywhere. Our own society is still, broadly speaking, liberal. To exercise your right of free speech you have to fight against economic pressure and against strong sections of public opinion, but not, as yet, against a secret police force. You can say or print almost anything so long as you are willing to do it in a hole-and-corner way. But what is sinister, as I said at the beginning of this essay, is that the conscious enemies of liberty are those to whom liberty ought to mean most. The big public do not care about the matter one way or the other. They are not in favor of persecuting the heretic, and they will not exert themselves to defend him. They are at once too sane and too stupid to acquire the totalitarian outlook. The direct, conscious attack on intellectual decency comes from the intellectuals themselves.

It is possible that the Russophile intelligentsia, if they had not succumbed to that particular myth, would have succumbed to another of much the same kind. But at any rate the Russian myth is there, and the corruption it causes stinks. When one sees highly educated men looking on indifferently at oppression and persecution, one wonders which to despise more, their cynicism or their short-sightedness. Many scientists, for example, are the uncritical admirers of the U.S.S.R. They appear to think that the destruction of liberty is of no importance so long as their own line of work is for the moment unaffected. The U.S.S.R. is a large, rapidly developing country which has acute need of scientific workers and, consequently, treats them generously. Provided that they steer clear of dangerous subjects such as psychology, scientists are privileged persons. Writers, on the other hand, are viciously persecuted. It is true that literary prostitutes like Ilya Ehrenburg or Alexei Tolstoy are paid huge sums of money, but the only thing which is of any value to the writer as such—his freedom of expression—is taken away from him. Some, at least, of the English scientists who speak so enthusiastically of the opportunities enjoyed by scientists in Russia are capable of understanding this. But their reflection appears to be: "Writers are persecuted in Russia. So what? I am not a writer." They do not see that any attack on intellectual liberty, and on the concept of objective truth, threatens in the long run every department of thought.

For the moment the totalitarian state tolerates the scientist because it needs him. Even in Nazi Germany, scientists, other than Jews, were relatively well treated and the German scientific community, as a whole, offered no resistance to Hitler. At this stage of history, even the most autocratic ruler is forced to take account of physical reality, partly because of the lingering-on of liberal habits of thought, partly because of the need to prepare for war. So long as physical reality cannot be altogether ignored, so long as two and two have to make four when you are, for example, drawing the blueprint of an aeroplane, the scientist has his function, and can even be allowed a measure of liberty. His awakening will come later, when the totalitarian state is firmly established. Meanwhile, if he wants to safeguard the integrity of science, it is his job to develop some kind of solidarity with his literary colleagues and not regard it as a matter of indifference when writers are silenced or driven to suicide, and newspapers systematically falsified.

But however it may be with the physical sciences, or with music, painting, and architecture, it is—as I have tried to show

—certain that literature is doomed if liberty of thought perishes. Not only is it doomed in any country which retains a totalitarian structure; but any writer who adopts the totalitarian outlook, who finds excuses for persecution and the falsification of reality, thereby destroys himself as a writer. There is no way out of this. No tirades against "individualism" and "the ivory tower," no pious platitudes to the effect that "true individuality is only attained through identification with the community," can get over the fact that a bought mind is a spoiled mind. Unless spontaneity enters at some point or another, literary creation is impossible, and language itself becomes ossified. At some time in the future, if the human mind becomes something totally different from what it now is, we may learn to separate literary creation from intellectual honesty. At present we know only that the imagination, like certain wild animals, will not breed in captivity. Any writer or journalist who denies that fact—and nearly all the current praise of the Soviet Union contains or implies such a denial—is, in effect, demanding his own destruction.

Second Thoughts
on James Burnham

JAMES BURNHAM'S BOOK, "THE MANAGERIAL REVOLUTION," MADE
a considerable stir both in the United States and in England
at the time when it was published, and its main thesis has
been so much discussed that a detailed exposition of it is
hardly necessary. As shortly as I can summarize it, the thesis
is this:

Capitalism is disappearing, but Socialism is not replacing
it. What is now arising is a new kind of planned, centralized
society which will be neither capitalist nor, in any accepted
sense of the word, democratic. The rulers of this new society
will be the people who effectively control the means of production: that is, business executives, technicians, bureaucrats, and
soldiers, lumped together by Burnham under the name of
"managers." These people will eliminate the old capitalistic
class, crush the working class, and so organize society that all
power and economic privilege remain in their own hands. Private property rights will be abolished, but common ownership
will not be established. The new "managerial" societies will
not consist of a patchwork of small, independent states, but of
great super-states grouped round the main industrial centres
in Europe, Asia, and America. These super-states will fight
among themselves for possession of the remaining uncaptured
portions of the earth, but will probably be unable to conquer

one another completely. Internally, each society will be hierarchical, with an aristocracy of talent at the top and a mass
of semi-slaves at the bottom.

In his next published book, *The Machiavellians,* Burnham
elaborates and also modifies his original statement. The greater
part of the book is an exposition of the theories of Machiavelli and of his modern disciples, Mosca, Michels and Pareto:
with doubtful justification, Burnham adds to these the syn-
dicalist writer, Georges Sorel. What Burnham is mainly concerned to show is that a democratic society has never existed
and, so far as we can see, never will exist. Society is of its nature
oligarchical, and the power of the oligarchy always rests upon
force and fraud. Burnham does not deny that "good" motives
may operate in private life, but he maintains that politics consists of the struggle for power, and nothing else. All historical
changes finally boil down to the replacement of one ruling
class by another. All talk about democracy, liberty, equality,
fraternity, all revolutionary movements, all visions of Utopia,
or "the classless society," or "the Kingdom of Heaven on
Earth," are humbug (not necessarily conscious humbug) covering the ambitions of some new class which is elbowing its way
into power. The English Puritans, the Jacobins, the Bol-
sheviks, were in each case simply power-seekers using the
hopes of the masses in order to win a privileged position for
themselves. Power can sometimes be won or maintained without violence, but never without fraud, because it is necessary
to make use of the masses, and the masses would not co-operate
if they knew that they were simply serving the purposes of a
minority. In each great revolutionary struggle the masses are
led on by vague dreams of human brotherhood, and then,
when the new ruling class is well established in power, they
are thrust back into servitude. This is practically the whole of
political history, as Burnham sees it.

Where the second book departs from the earlier one is in
asserting that the whole process could be somewhat moralized
if the facts were faced more honestly. *The Machiavellians* is
sub-titled "Defenders of Freedom." Machiavelli and his followers taught that in politics decency simply does not exist and,
by doing so, Burnham claims, made it possible to conduct political affairs more intelligently and less oppressively. A ruling
class which recognized that its real aim was to stay in power
would also recognize that it would be more likely to succeed
if it served the common good, and might avoid stiffening into
a hereditary aristocracy. Burnham lays much stress on Pareto's
theory of the "circulation of the élites." If it is to stay in power
a ruling class must constantly admit suitable recruits from
below, so that the ablest men may always be at the top and a
new class of power-hungry malcontents cannot come into
being. This is likeliest to happen, Burnham considers, in a
society which retains democratic habits—that is, where opposition is permitted and certain bodies such as the Press and the
trade unions can keep their autonomy. Here Burnham un-
doubtedly contradicts his earlier opinion. In *The Managerial
Revolution,* which was written in 1940, it is taken as a matter
of course that "managerial" Germany is in all ways more efficient than a capitalist democracy such as France or Britain. In
the second book, written in 1942, Burnham admits that the
Germans might have avoided some of their more serious stra-
tegic errors if they had permitted freedom of speech. However,
the main thesis is not abandoned. Capitalism is doomed, and
Socialism is a dream. If we grasp what is at issue we may guide
the course of the managerial revolution to some extent, but
that revolution is *happening,* whether we like it or not. In
both books, but especially the earlier one, there is a note of
unmistakable relish over the cruelty and wickedness of the
processes that are being discussed. Although he reiterates that

he is merely setting forth the facts and not stating his own preferences, it is clear that Burnham is fascinated by the spectacle of power, and that his sympathies were with Germany so long as Germany appeared to be winning the war. A more recent essay, "Lenin's Heir," published in the *Partisan Review* about the beginning of 1945, suggests that this sympathy has since been transferred to the U.S.S.R. "Lenin's Heir" provoked violent controversy in the American left-wing press; I must return to it later.

It will be seen that Burnham's theory is not, strictly speaking, a new one. Many earlier writers have foreseen the emergence of a new kind of society, neither capitalist nor Socialist, and probably based upon slavery: though most of them have differed from Burnham in not assuming this development to be *inevitable*. A good example is Hilaire Belloc's book, *The Servile State*, published in 1911. *The Servile State* is written in a tiresome style, and the remedy it suggests (a return to small-scale peasant ownership) is for many reasons impossible: still, it does foretell with remarkable insight the kind of things that have been happening from about 1930 onwards. Chesterton, in a less methodical way, predicted the disappearance of democracy and private property, and the rise of a slave society which might be called either capitalist or Communist. Jack London, in *The Iron Heel* (1909), foretold some of the essential features of Fascism, and such books as Wells' *The Sleeper Awakes* (1900), Zamyatin's *We* (1923), and Aldous Huxley's *Brave New World* (1930), all described imaginary worlds in which the special problems of capitalism had been solved without bringing liberty, equality, or true happiness any nearer. More recently, writers like Peter Drucker and F. A. Voigt have argued that Fascism and Communism are substantially the same thing. And indeed, it has always been obvious that a planned and centralized society is liable to develop into an oligarchy or a dictatorship. Orthodox Conservatives were unable to see this, because it comforted them to assume that Socialism "wouldn't work," and that the disappearance of capitalism would mean chaos and anarchy. Orthodox Socialists could not see it, because they wished to think that they themselves would soon be in power, and therefore assumed that when capitalism disappears, Socialism takes its place. As a result they were unable to foresee the rise of Fascism, or to make correct predictions about it after it had appeared. Later, the need to justify the Russian dictatorship and to explain away the obvious resemblances between Communism and Nazism clouded the issue still more. But the notion that industrialism must end in monopoly, and that monopoly must imply tyranny is not a startling one.

Where Burnham differs from most other thinkers is in trying to plot the course of the "managerial revolution" accurately on a world scale, and in assuming that the drift towards totalitarianism is irresistible and must not be fought against, though it may be guided. According to Burnham, writing in 1940, "managerialism" has reached its fullest development in the U.S.S.R. but is almost equally well developed in Germany, and has made its appearance in the United States. He describes the New Deal as "primitive managerialism." But the trend is the same everywhere, or almost everywhere. Always *laissez-faire* capitalism gives way to planning and State interference, the mere *owner* loses power as against the technician and the bureaucrat, but Socialism—that is to say, what used to be called Socialism—shows no sign of emerging:

Some apologists try to excuse Marxism by saying that it has "never had a chance." This is far from the truth. Marxism and the Marxist parties have had dozens of chances. In *Russia* a Marxist party took power. Within a short time it abandoned Socialism; if not in words, at any rate in the effect of its actions. In most European nations there were during the last months of the first world war and the years immediately thereafter, social crises which left a wide-open door for the Marxist parties: without exception they proved unable to take and hold power. In a large number of countries—*Germany, Denmark, Norway, Sweden, Austria, England, Australia, New Zealand, Spain, France*—the reformist Marxist parties have administered the governments, and have uniformly failed to introduce Socialism or make any genuine step towards Socialism. . . . These parties have, in practice, at every historical test—and there have been many—either failed Socialism or abandoned it. This is the fact which neither the bitterest foe nor the most ardent friend of Socialism can erase. This fact does not, as some think, prove anything about the moral quality of the Socialist ideal. But it does constitute unblinkable evidence that, whatever its moral quality, Socialism is not going to come.

Burnham does not, of course, deny that the new "managerial" régimes, like the régimes of Russia and Nazi Germany, may be *called* Socialist. He means merely that they will not *be* Socialist in any sense of the word which would have been accepted by Marx, or Lenin, or Keir Hardie, or William Morris, or indeed, by any representative Socialist prior to about 1930. Socialism, until recently, was supposed to connote political democracy, social equality, and internationalism. There is not the smallest sign that any of these things is in a way to being established anywhere, and the one great country in which something described as a proletarian revolution once happened, i.e. the U.S.S.R., has moved steadily away from the old concept of a free and equal society aiming at universal human brotherhood. In an almost unbroken progress since the early days of the Revolution, liberty has been chipped away and representative institutions smothered, while inequalities have increased and nationalism and militarism have grown stronger. But at the same time, Burnham insists, there has been no tendency to return to capitalism. What is happening is simply the growth of "managerialism," which, according to Burnham, is in progress everywhere, though the manner in which it comes about may vary from country to country.

Now, as an interpretation of what *is happening,* Burnham's theory is extremely plausible, to put it at the lowest. The events of, at any rate, the last fifteen years in the U.S.S.R. can be far more easily explained by this theory than by any other. Evidently the U.S.S.R. is not Socialist, and can only be called Socialist if one gives the word a meaning different from what it would have in any other context. On the other hand, prophecies that the Russian régime would revert to capitalism have always been falsified, and now seem further than ever from being fulfilled. In claiming that the process had gone almost equally far in Nazi Germany Burnham probably exaggerates, but it seems certain that the drift was away from old-style capitalism and towards a planned economy with an adoptive oligarchy in control. In Russia the capitalists were destroyed first and the workers were crushed later. In Germany the workers were crushed first, but the elimination of the capitalists had at any rate begun, and calculations based on the assumption that Nazism was "simply capitalism" were always contradicted by events. Where Burnham seems to go most astray is in believing "managerialism" to be on the up-grade in the United States, the one great country where free capitalism is still vigorous. But if one considers the world-movement as a whole, his conclusions are difficult to resist; and even in the United States the all-prevailing faith in *laissez-faire* may not survive the next great economic crisis. It has been urged against Burnham that he assigns far too much importance to the "managers," in the narrow sense of the word—that is, factory bosses, planners, and technicians—and seems to assume that even in Soviet Russia it is these people, and not the Communist Party chiefs, who are the real holders of power. How-

ever, this is a secondary error, and it is partially corrected in
The Machiavellians. The real question is not whether the people who wipe their boots on us during the next fifty years are
to be called managers, bureaucrats, or politicians: the question
is whether capitalism, now obviously doomed, is to give way
to oligarchy or to true democracy.

But curiously enough, when one examines the predictions
which Burnham has based on his general theory, one finds that
in so far as they are verifiable, they have been falsified. Numbers of people have pointed this out already. However, it is
worth following up Burnham's predictions in detail, because
they form a sort of pattern which is related to contemporary
events, and which reveals, I believe, a very important weakness in present-day political thought.

To begin with, writing in 1940, Burnham takes a German
victory more or less for granted. Britain is described as "dissolving," and as displaying "all the characteristics which have
distinguished decadent cultures in past historical transitions,"
while the conquest and integration of Europe which Germany
achieved in 1940 is described as "irreversible." "England,"
writes Burnham, "no matter with what non-European allies,
cannot conceivably hope to conquer the European continent."
Even if Germany should somehow manage to lose the war, she
could not be dismembered or reduced to the status of the Wei-
mar Republic, but is bound to remain as the nucleus of a
unified Europe. The future map of the world, with its three
great super-states is, in any case, already settled in its main outlines: and "the nuclei of these great super-states are, whatever
may be their future names, the previously existing nations,
Japan, Germany, and the United States."

Burnham also commits himself to the opinion that Germany
will not attack the U.S.S.R. until after Britain has been defeated. In a condensation of his book published in the *Partisan*

Review of May-June, 1941, and presumably written later than
the book itself, he says:

> As in the case of *Russia*, so with *Germany*, the third part of the
> managerial problem—the contest for dominance with other sections
> of managerial society—remains for the future. First had to come the
> death blow that assured the toppling of the capitalist world order,
> which meant above all the destruction of the foundations of the
> *British Empire* (the keystone of the capitalist world order) both di-
> rectly and through the smashing of the European political structure,
> which was a necessary prop of the Empire. This is the basic explana-
> tion of the Nazi-Soviet Pact, which is not intelligible on other
> grounds. The future conflict between *Germany* and *Russia* will be
> a managerial conflict proper; prior to the great world managerial
> battles, the end of the capitalist order must be assured. The belief
> that Nazism is "decadent capitalism" . . . makes it impossible to
> explain reasonably the Nazi-Soviet Pact. From this belief followed
> the always expected war between *Germany* and *Russia*, not the ac-
> tual war to the death between *Germany* and the *British Empire*. The
> war between *Germany* and *Russia* is one of the managerial wars of
> the future, not of the anti-capitalist wars of yesterday and today.

However, the attack on Russia will come later, and Russia is
certain, or almost certain, to be defeated. "There is every reason to believe . . . that Russia will split apart, with the western
half gravitating towards the European base and the eastern towards the Asiatic." This quotation comes from *The Managerial Revolution*. In the above-quoted article, written probably
about six months later, it is put more forcibly: "The Russian
weaknesses indicate that Russia will not be able to endure, that
it will crack apart, and fall towards east and west." And in a
supplementary note which was added to the English (Pelican)
edition, and which appears to have been written at the end of
1941, Burnham speaks as though the "cracking apart" process
were already happening. The war, he says, "is part of the
means whereby the western half of Russia is being integrated
into the European super-state."

Sorting these various statements out, we have the following prophecies:

1. Germany is bound to win the war.
2. Germany and Japan are bound to survive as great states, and to remain the nuclei of power in their respective areas.
3. Germany will not attack the U.S.S.R. until after the defeat of Britain.
4. The U.S.S.R. is bound to be defeated.

However, Burnham has made other predictions besides these. In a short article in the *Partisan Review*, in the summer of 1944, he gives his opinion that the U.S.S.R. will gang up with Japan in order to prevent the total defeat of the latter, while the American Communists will be set to work to sabotage the eastern end of the war. And finally, in an article in the same magazine in the winter of 1944-45, he claims that Russia, destined so short a while ago to "crack apart," is within sight of conquering the whole of Eurasia. This article was the cause of violent controversies among the American intelligentsia. I must give some account of it here, because its manner of approach and its emotional tone are of a peculiar kind, and by studying them one can get nearer to the real roots of Burnham's theory.

The article is entitled "Lenin's Heir," and it sets out to show that Stalin is the true and legitimate guardian of the Russian Revolution, which he has not in any sense "betrayed" but has merely carried forward on lines that were implicit in it from the start. In itself, this is an easier opinion to swallow than the usual Trotskyist claim that Stalin is a mere crook who has perverted the Revolution to his own ends, and that things would somehow have been different if Lenin had lived or Trotsky had remained in power. Actually there is no strong reason for thinking that the main lines of development would have been very different. Well before 1923 the seeds of a totalitarian society were quite plainly there. Lenin, indeed, is one of those politicians who win an undeserved reputation by dying prematurely.[1] Had he lived, it is probable that he would either have been thrown out, like Trotsky, or would have kept himself in power by methods as barbarous, or nearly as barbarous, as those of Stalin. The *title* of Burnham's essay, therefore, sets forth a reasonable thesis, and one would expect him to support it by an appeal to the facts.

However, the essay barely touches upon its ostensible subject-matter. It is obvious that anyone genuinely concerned to show that there has been continuity of policy as between Lenin and Stalin, would start by outlining Lenin's policy and then explain in what way Stalin's has resembled it. Burnham does not do this. Except for one or two cursory sentences he says nothing about Lenin's policy, and Lenin's name only occurs five times in an essay of twelve pages: in the first seven pages, apart from the title, it does not occur at all. The real aim of the essay is to present Stalin as a towering super-human figure, indeed a species of demigod, and Bolshevism as an irresistible force which is flowing over the earth and cannot be halted until it reaches the outermost borders of Eurasia. In so far as he makes any attempt to prove his case, Burnham does so by repeating over and over again that Stalin is "a great man"—which is probably true, but is almost completely irrelevant. Moreover, though he does advance some solid arguments for believing in Stalin's genius, it is clear that in his

[1] It is difficult to think of any politician who has lived to be eighty and still been regarded as a success. What we call a "great" statesman normally means one who dies before his policy has had time to take effect. If Cromwell had lived a few years longer he would probably have fallen from power, in which case we should now regard him as a failure. If Pétain had died in 1930, France would have venerated him as a hero and patriot. Napoleon remarked once that if only a cannon ball had happened to hit him when he was riding into Moscow, he would have gone down to history as the greatest man who ever lived.

mind the idea of "greatness" is inextricably mixed up with
the idea of cruelty and dishonesty. There are curious passages
in which it seems to be suggested that Stalin is to be admired
because of the limitless suffering that he has caused:

Stalin proves himself a "great man," in the grand style. The accounts of the banquets, staged in Moscow for the visiting dignitaries,
set the symbolic tone. With their enormous menus of sturgeon, and
roasts, and fowl, and sweets; their streams of liquor; the scores of
toasts with which they end; the silent, unmoving secret police behind each guest; all against the winter background of the starving
multitudes of besieged *Leningrad;* the dying millions at the front;
the jammed concentration camps; the city crowds kept by their
minute rations just at the edge of life; there is little trace of dull
mediocrity or the hand of *Babbitt.* We recognize, rather, the tradition of the most spectacular of the Tsars, of the Great Kings of the
Medes and Persians, of the Khanate of the Golden Horde, of the
banquet we assign to the gods of the Heroic Ages in tribute to the
insight that insolence, and indifference, and brutality on such a scale
remove beings from the human level. . . . *Stalin's* political tech-
niques show a freedom from conventional restrictions that is incompatible with mediocrity: the mediocre man is custom-bound. Often
it is the scale of his operations that sets them apart. It is usual, for
example, for men active in practical life to engineer an occasional
frame-up. But to carry out a frame-up against tens of thousands of
persons, important percentages of whole strata of society, including
most of one's own comrades, is so far out of the ordinary that the
long-run mass conclusion is either that the frame-up must be true—
at least "have some truth in it"—or that power so immense must be
submitted to—is an "historical necessity," as intellectuals put it. . . .
There is nothing unexpected in letting a few individuals starve for
reasons of state; but to starve, by deliberate decision, several millions
is a type of action attributed ordinarily only to gods.

In these and other similar passages there may be a tinge
of irony, but it is difficult not to feel that there is also a sort
of fascinated admiration. Towards the end of the essay Burnham compares Stalin with those semi-mythical heroes, like

Moses or Asoka, who embody in themselves a whole epoch,
and can justly be credited with feats that they did not actually
perform. In writing of Soviet foreign policy and its supposed
objectives, he touches an even more mystical note:

> Starting from the magnetic core of the Eurasian heartland, the
> Soviet power, like the reality of the One of Neo-Platonism overflow-
> ing in the descending series of the emanative progression, flows out-
> ward, west into Europe, south into the Near East, east into China,
> already lapping the shores of the Atlantic, the Yellow and China
> Seas, the Mediterranean, and the Persian Gulf. As the undifferen-
> tiated One, in its progression, descends through the stages of Mind,
> Soul, and Matter, and then through its fatal Return back to itself;
> so does the Soviet power, emanating from the integrally totalitarian
> center, proceed outwards by Absorption (the Baltics, Bessarabia,
> Bukovina, East Poland), Domination (Finland, the Balkans, Mon-
> golia, North China and, tomorrow, Germany), Orienting Influence
> (Italy, France, Turkey, Iran, Central and South China . . .), until
> it is dissipated in MHON, the outer material sphere, beyond the
> Eurasian boundaries, of momentary Appeasement and Infiltration
> (England, the United States).

I do not think it is fanciful to suggest that the unnecessary
capital letters with which this passage is loaded are intended
to have a hypnotic effect on the reader. Burnham is trying to
build up a picture of terrifying, irresistible power, and to turn
a normal political maneuver like infiltration into Infiltration
adds to the general portentousness. The essay should be read
in full. Although it is not the kind of tribute that the average
Russophile would consider acceptable, and although Burnham
himself would probably claim that he is being strictly objective, he is in effect performing an act of homage, and even
of self-abasement. Meanwhile, this essay gives us another
prophecy to add to the list: i.e. that the U.S.S.R. will conquer
the whole of Eurasia, and probably a great deal more. And
one must remember that Burnham's basic theory contains in

itself, a prediction which still has to be tested—that is, that whatever else happens, the "managerial" form of society is bound to prevail.

Burnham's earlier prophecy, of a German victory in the war and the integration of Europe round the German nucleus, was falsified, not only in its main outlines, but in some important details. Burnham insists all the way through that "managerialism" is not only more efficient than capitalist democracy or Marxian Socialism, but also more acceptable to the masses. The slogans of democracy and national self-determination, he says, no longer have any mass appeal: "managerialism," on the other hand, can rouse enthusiasm, produce intelligible war aims, establish fifth columns everywhere, and inspire its soldiers with a fanatical morale. The "fanaticism" of the Germans, as against the "apathy" or "indifference" of the British, French, etc., is much emphasized, and Nazism is represented as a revolutionary force sweeping across Europe and spreading its philosophy "by contagion." The Nazi fifth columns "cannot be wiped out," and the democratic nations are quite incapable of projecting any settlement which the German or other European masses would prefer to the New Order. In any case, the democracies can only defeat Germany if they go "still further along the managerial road than Germany has yet gone."

The germ of truth in all this is that the smaller European states, demoralized by the chaos and stagnation of the pre-war years, collapsed rather more quickly than they need have done, and might conceivably have accepted the New Order if the Germans had kept some of their promises. But the actual experience of German rule aroused almost at once such a fury of hatred and vindictiveness as the world has seldom seen. After about the beginning of 1941 there was hardly any need of a positive war aim, since getting rid of the Germans was a sufficient objective. The question of morale, and its relation to national solidarity, is a nebulous one, and the evidence can be so manipulated as to prove almost anything. But if one goes by the proportion of prisoners to other casualties, and the amount of quislingism, the totalitarian states come out of the comparison worse than the democracies. Hundreds of thousands of Russians appear to have gone over to the Germans during the course of the war, while comparable numbers of Germans and Italians had gone over to the allies before the war started: the corresponding number of American or British renegades would have amounted to a few scores. As an example of the inability of "capitalist ideologies" to enlist support, Burnham cites, "the complete failure of voluntary military recruiting in England [as well as the entire British Empire] and in the United States." One would gather from this that the armies of the totalitarian states were manned by volunteers. Actually, no totalitarian state has ever so much as considered voluntary recruitment for any purpose, nor, throughout history, has a large army ever been raised by voluntary means.[1] It is not worth listing the many similar arguments that Burnham puts forward. The point is that he assumes that the Germans must win the propaganda war as well as the military one, and that, at any rate in Europe, this estimate was not borne out by events.

It will be seen that Burnham's predictions have not merely, when they were verifiable, turned out to be wrong, but that they have sometimes contradicted one another in a sensa-

---

[1] Great Britain raised a million volunteers in the earlier part of the 1914-18 war. This must be a world's record, but the pressures applied were such that it is doubtful whether the recruitment ought to be described as voluntary. Even the most "ideological" wars have been fought largely by pressed men. In the English civil war, the Napoleonic wars, the American civil war, the Spanish civil war, etc., both sides resorted to conscription or the press gang.

tional way. It is this last fact that is significant. Political predictions are usually wrong, because they are usually based on
wish-thinking, but they can have symptomatic value, especially
when they change abruptly. Often the revealing factor is the
date at which they are made. Dating Burnham's various writings as accurately as can be done from internal evidence, and
then noting what events they coincided with, we find the following relationships:

In *The Managerial Revolution* Burnham prophesies a
German victory, postponement of the Russo-German war
until after Britain is defeated and, subsequently, the defeat
of Russia. The book, or much of it, was written in the second
half of 1940—i.e. at a time when the Germans had overrun
Western Europe and were bombing Britain, and the Russians
were collaborating with them fairly closely, and in what appeared, at any rate, to be a spirit of appeasement.

In the supplementary note added to the English edition of
the book, Burnham appears to assume that the U.S.S.R. is
already beaten and the splitting-up process is about to begin.
This was published in the spring of 1942 and presumably
written at the end of 1941; i.e. when the Germans were in the
suburbs of Moscow.

The prediction that Russia would gang up with Japan
against the U.S.A. was written early in 1944, soon after the
conclusion of a new Russo-Japanese treaty.

The prophecy of Russian world-conquest was written in
the winter of 1944, when the Russians were advancing rapidly in Eastern Europe while the Western Allies were still
held up in Italy and northern France.

It will be seen that at each point Burnham is predicting
a continuation of the thing that is happening. Now the tendency to do this is not simply a bad habit, like inaccuracy or
exaggeration, which one can correct by taking thought. It is

a major mental disease, and its roots lie partly in cowardice and partly in the worship of power, which is not fully separable from cowardice.

Suppose in 1940 you had taken a Gallup poll, in England, on the question, "Will Germany win the war?" You would have found, curiously enough, that the group answering "Yes" contained a far higher percentage of intelligent people—people with I.Q.s of over 120, shall we say—than the group answering "No." The same would have held good in the middle of 1942. In this case the figures would not have been so striking but if you had made the question, "Will the Germans capture Alexandria?" or "Will the Japanese be able to hold on to the territories they have captured?" then once again there would have been a very marked tendency for intelligence to concentrate in the "Yes" group. In every case the less gifted person would have been likelier to give a right answer.

If one went simply by these instances, one might assume that high in.elligence and bad military judgment always go together. However, it is not so simple as that. The English intelligentsia, on the whole, were more defeatist than the mass of the people—and some of them went on being defeatist at a time when the war was quite plainly won—partly because they were better able to visualize the dreary years of warfare that lay ahead. Their morale was worse because their imaginations were stronger. The quickest way of ending a war is to lose it, and if one finds the prospect of a long war intolerable, it is natural to disbelieve in the possibility of victory. But there was more to it than that. There was also the disaffection of large numbers of intellectuals which made it difficult for them not to side with any country hostile to Britain. And the deepest of all, there was admiration—though only in a very few cases conscious admiration—for the power, energy, and cruelty of the Nazi régime. It would be a useful though tedious labor to go through the Left-wing Press and enumerate all the hostile references to Nazism during the years 1935-45. One would find, I have little doubt, that they reached their high-water mark in 1937-8 and 1944-5, and dropped off noticeably in the years 1939-42—that is, during the period when Germany seemed to be winning. One would find, also the same people advocating a compromise peace in 1940 and approving the dismemberment of Germany in 1945. And if one studied the reactions of the English intelligentsia towards the U.S.S.R., there, too, one would find genuinely progressive impulses mixed up with admiration for power and cruelty. It would be grossly unfair to suggest that power-worship is the only motive for Russophile feeling, but it is one motive, and among intellectuals it is probably the strongest one.

Power-worship blurs political judgment because it leads, almost unavoidably, to the belief that present trends will continue. Whoever is winning at the moment will always seem to be invincible. If the Japanese have conquered South Asia, then they will keep South Asia for ever; if the Germans have captured Tobruk, they will infallibly capture Cairo; if the Russians are in Berlin, it will not be long before they are in London: and so on. This habit of mind leads also to the belief that things will happen more quickly, completely, and catastrophically than they ever do in practice. The rise and fall of empires, the disappearance of cultures and religions, are expected to happen with earthquake suddenness, and processes which have barely started are talked about as though they were already at an end. Burnham's writings are full of apocalyptic visions. Nations, governments, classes, and social systems are constantly described as expanding, contracting, decaying, dissolving, toppling, crashing, crumbling, crystallizing and, in general, behaving in an unstable and melodramatic way. The slowness of historical change, the fact that any epoch always contains a great deal of the last epoch, is never sufficiently allowed for. Such a manner of thinking is bound to lead to mistaken prophecies, because, even when it gauges the direction of events rightly, it will miscalculate their tempo. Within the space of five years Burnham foretold the domination of Russia by Germany and of Germany by Russia. In each case he was obeying the same instinct: the instinct to bow down before the conqueror of the moment, to accept the existing trend as irreversible. With this in mind one can criticize his theory in a broader way.

The mistakes I have pointed out do not disprove Burnham's theory, but they do cast light on his probable reasons for holding it. In this connection one cannot leave out of account the fact that Burnham is an American. Every political theory has a certain regional tinge about it, and every nation, every culture, has its own characteristic prejudices and patches of ignorance. There are certain problems that must almost inevitably be seen in a different perspective according to the geographical situation from which one is looking at them. Now, the attitude that Burnham adopts, of classifying Communism and Fascism as much the same thing, and at the same time accepting both of them—or, at any rate, not assuming that either must be violently struggled against—is essentially an American attitude, and would be almost impossible for an Englishman or any other western European. English writers who consider Communism and Fascism to be *the same thing*, invariably hold that both are monstrous evils which must be fought to the death: on the other hand, any Englishman who believes Communism and Fascism to be opposites will feel that he ought to side with one or the other.[1] The reason

[1] The only exception I am able to think of is Bernard Shaw, who, for some years at any rate, declared Communism and Fascism to be much the same thing, and was in favor of both of them. But Shaw, after all, is not

for this difference of outlook is simple enough and, as usual, is bound up with wish-thinking. If totalitarianism triumphs and the dreams of the geo-politicians come true, Britain will disappear as a world power and the whole of western Europe will be swallowed by some single great state. This is not a prospect that it is easy for an Englishman to contemplate with detachment. Either he does not want Britain to disappear—in which case he will tend to construct theories proving the thing that he wants—or like a minority of intellectuals, he will decide that his country is finished and transfer his allegiance to some foreign power. An American does not have to make the same choice. Whatever happens, the United States will survive as a great power, and from the American point of view it does not make much difference whether Europe is dominated by Russia or by Germany. Most Americans who think of the matter at all would prefer to see the world divided between two or three monster states which had reached their natural boundaries and could bargain with one another on economic issues without being troubled by ideological differences. Such a world-picture fits in with the American tendency to admire size for its own sake and to feel that success constitutes justification, and it fits in with the all-prevailing anti-British sentiment. In practice, Britain and the United States have twice been forced into alliance against Germany, and will probably, before long, be forced into alliance against Russia: but, subjectively, a majority of Americans would prefer either Russia or Germany to Britain and, as between Russia and Germany, would prefer whichever seemed stronger at the moment.[1] It is, therefore, not surprising that Burnham's

an Englishman, and probably does not feel his fate to be bound up with that of Britain.

[1] As late as the autumn of 1945, a Gallup poll taken among the American troops in Germany showed that 51 per cent "thought Hitler did much

world-view should often be noticeably close to that of the American imperialists on the one side, or to that of the isolationists on the other. It is a "tough" or "realistic" world-view which fits in with the American form of wish-thinking. The almost open admiration for Nazi methods which Burnham shows in the earlier of his two books, and which would seem shocking to almost any English reader, depends ultimately on the fact that the Atlantic is wider than the Channel.

As I have said earlier, Burnham has probably been more right than wrong about the present and the immediate past. For quite fifty years past the general drift has almost certainly been towards oligarchy. The ever-increasing concentration of industrial and financial power; the diminishing importance of the individual capitalist or shareholder, and the growth of the new "managerial" class of scientists, technicians, and bureaucrats; the weakness of the proletariat against the centralized state; the increasing helplessness of small countries against big ones; the decay of representative institutions and the appearance of one-party régimes based on police terrorism, faked plebiscites, etc.: all these things seem to point in the same direction. Burnham sees the trend and assumes that it is irresistible, rather as a rabbit fascinated by a boa constrictor might assume that a boa constrictor is the strongest thing in the world. When one looks a little deeper, one sees that all his ideas rest upon two axioms which are taken for granted in the earlier book and made partly explicit in the second one. They are:

(a) Politics is essentially the same in all ages.
(b) Political behavior is different from other kinds of behavior.

good before 1939." This was after five years of anti-Hitler propaganda. The verdict, as quoted, is not very strongly favorable to Germany, but it is hard to believe that a verdict equally favorable to Britain would be given by anywhere near 51 per cent of the American Army.

To take the second point first. In *The Machiavellians,* Burnham insists that politics is simply the struggle for power. Every great social movement, every war, every revolution, every political program, however edifying and Utopian, really has behind it the ambitions of some sectional group which is out to grab power for itself. Power can never be restrained by any ethical or religious code, but only by other power. The nearest possible approach to altruistic behavior is the perception by a ruling group that it will probably stay in power longer if it behaves decently. But curiously enough, these generalizations only apply to political behavior, not to any other kind of behavior. In everyday life, as Burnham sees and admits, one cannot explain every human action by applying the principle of *cui bono?* Obviously human beings have impulses which are not selfish. Man, therefore, is an animal that can act morally when he acts as an individual, but becomes unmoral when he acts collectively. But even this generalization only holds good for the higher groups. The masses, it seems, have vague aspirations towards liberty and human brotherhood, which are easily played upon by power-hungry individuals and minorities. So that history consists of a series of swindles, in which the masses are first lured into revolt by the promise of Utopia, and then, when they have done their job, enslaved over again by new masters.

Political activity, therefore, is a special kind of behavior, characterized by its complete unscrupulousness and occurring only among small groups of the population, especially among dissatisfied groups whose talents do not get free play under the existing form of society. The great mass of the people—and this is where (b) ties up with (a)—will always be unpolitical. In effect, therefore, humanity is divided into two classes: the self-seeking, hypocritical minority, and the brainless mob whose destiny is always to be led or driven, as one

gets a pig back to the sty by kicking it on the bottom or by
rattling a stick inside a swill-bucket, according to the needs
of the moment. And this beautiful pattern is to continue
for ever. Individuals may pass from one category to another,
whole classes may destroy other classes and rise to the dominant position, but the division of humanity into rulers and
ruled is unalterable. In their capabilities, as in their desires
and needs, men are not equal. There is an "iron law of
oligarchy," which would operate even if democracy were not
impossible for mechanical reasons.

It is curious that in all his talk about the struggle for power,
Burnham never stops to ask *why* people want power. He
seems to assume that power-hunger, although only dominant
in comparatively few people, is a natural instinct that does
not have to be explained, like the desire for food. He also
assumes that the division of society into classes serves the
same purpose in all ages. This is practically to ignore the history of hundreds of years. When Burnham's master, Machiavelli, was writing, class divisions were not only unavoidable,
but desirable. So long as methods of production were primitive, the great mass of the people were necessarily tied down
to dreary, exhausting manual labor: and a few people had to
be set free from such labor, otherwise civilization could not
maintain itself, let alone make any progress. But since the
arrival of the machine the whole pattern has altered. The justification for class distinctions, if there is a justification, is no
longer the same, because there is no mechanical reason why
the average human being should continue to be a drudge.
True, drudgery persists; class distinctions are probably re-
establishing themselves in a new form, and individual liberty
is on the down-grade: but as these developments are now
technically avoidable, they must have some psychological
cause which Burnham makes no attempt to discover. The

question that he ought to ask, and never does ask, is: why does the lust for naked power become a major human motive exactly *now*, when the dominion of man over man is ceasing to be necessary? As for the claim that "human nature," or "inexorable laws" of this and that, make Socialism impossible, it is simply a projection of the past into the future. In effect, Burnham argues that because a society of free and equal human beings has never existed, it never can exist. By the same argument one could have demonstrated the impossibility of aeroplanes in 1900, or of motor cars in 1850.

The notion that the machine has altered human relationships, and that in consequence Machiavelli is out of date, is a very obvious one. If Burnham fails to deal with it, it can, I think, only be because his own power-instinct leads him to brush aside any suggestion that the Machiavellian world of force, fraud, and tyranny may somehow come to an end. It is important to bear in mind what I said above: that Burnham's theory is only a variant—an American variant, and interesting because of its comprehensiveness—of the power-worship now so prevalent among intellectuals. A more normal variant, at any rate in England, is Communism. If one examines the people who, having some idea of what the Russian régime is like, are strongly Russophile, one finds that, on the whole, they belong to the "managerial" class of which Burnham writes. That is, they are not managers in the narrow sense, but scientists, technicians, teachers, journalists, broadcasters, bureaucrats, professional politicians: in general, middling people who feel themselves cramped by a system that is still partly aristocratic, and are hungry for more power and more prestige. These people look towards the U.S.S.R. and see in it, or think they see, a system which eliminates the upper class, keeps the working class in its place, and hands unlimited power to people very similar to themselves. It was only *after*

the Soviet régime became unmistakably totalitarian that English intellectuals, in large numbers, began to show an interest
in it. Burnham, although the English Russophile intelligentsia
would repudiate him, is really voicing their secret wish: the
wish to destroy the old, equalitarian version of Socialism and
usher in a hierarchical society where the intellectual can at
last get his hands on the whip. Burnham at least has the honesty to say that Socialism isn't coming; the others merely say
that Socialism *is* coming, and then give the word "Socialism"
a new meaning which makes nonsense of the old one. But his
theory, for all its appearance of objectivity, is the rationaliza-
tion of a wish. There is no strong reason for thinking that it
tells us anything about the future, except perhaps the immediate future. It merely tells us what kind of world the
"managerial" class themselves, or at least the more conscious
and ambitious members of the class, would like to live in.

Fortunately the "managers" are not so invincible as Burnham believes. It is curious how persistently, in *The Managerial Revolution,* he ignores the advantages, military as well
as social, enjoyed by a democratic country. At every point the
evidence is squeezed in order to show the strength, vitality,
and durability of Hitler's crazy régime. Germany is expanding
rapidly, and "rapid territorial expansion has always been a
sign not of decadence . . . but of renewal." Germany makes
war successfully, and "the ability to make war well is never a
sign of decadence but of its opposite." Germany also "inspires
in millions of persons a fanatical loyalty. This, too, never
accompanies decadence." Even the cruelty and dishonesty of
the Nazi régime are cited in its favor, since "the young, new,
rising social order is, as against the old, more likely to resort
on a large scale to lies, terror, persecution." Yet, within only
five years this young, rising social order had smashed itself to
pieces and become, in Burnham's usage of the word, deca-

dent. And this had happened quite largely because of the "managerial" (i.e. undemocratic) structure which Burnham admires. The immediate cause of the German defeat was the unheard-of folly of attacking the U.S.S.R. while Britain was still undefeated and America was manifestly getting ready to fight. Mistakes of this magnitude can only be made, or at any rate they are most likely to be made, in countries where public opinion has no power. So long as the common man can get a hearing, such elementary rules as not fighting all your enemies simultaneously are less likely to be violated.

But, in any case, one should have been able to see from the start that such a movement as Nazism could not produce any good or stable result. Actually, so long as they were winning, Burnham seems to have seen nothing wrong with the methods of the Nazis. Such methods, he says, only appear wicked because they are new:

> There is no historical law that polite manners and "justice" shall conquer. In history there is always the question of *whose* manners and *whose* justice. A rising social class and a new order of society have got to break through the old moral codes just as they must break through the old economic and political institutions. Naturally, from the point of view of the old, they are monsters. If they win, they take care in due time of manners and morals.

This implies that literally anything can become right or wrong if the dominant class of the moment so wills it. It ignores the fact that certain rules of conduct have to be observed if human society is to hold together at all. Burnham, therefore, was unable to see that the crimes and follies of the Nazi régime *must* lead by one route or another to disaster. So also with his new-found admiration for Stalinism. It is too early to say in just what way the Russian régime will destroy itself. If I had to make a prophecy, I should say that a continuation of the Russian policies of the last fifteen years—and internal and external policy, of course, are merely two facets of the same thing—can only lead to a war conducted with atomic bombs, which will make Hitler's invasion look like a tea-party. But at any rate, the Russian régime will either democratize itself, or it will perish. The huge, invincible, ever-lasting slave empire of which Burnham appears to dream will not be established or, if established, will not endure, because slavery is no longer a stable basis for human society.

One cannot always make positive prophecies, but there are times when one ought to be able to make negative ones. No one could have been expected to foresee the exact results of the Treaty of Versailles, but millions of thinking people could and did foresee that those results would be bad. Plenty of people, though not so many in this case, can foresee that the results of the settlement now being forced on Europe will also be bad. And to refrain from admiring Hitler or Stalin—that, too, should not require an enormous intellectual effort. But it is partly a moral effort. That a man of Burnham's gifts should have been able for a while to think of Nazism as something rather admirable, something that could and probably would build up a workable and durable social order, shows what damage is done to the sense of reality by the cultivation of what is now called "realism."

I Write as I Please

The Sporting Spirit

NOW THAT THE BRIEF VISIT OF THE DYNAMO FOOTBALL TEAM [1]
has come to an end, it is possible to say publicly what many
thinking people were saying privately before the Dynamos
ever arrived. That is, that sport is an unfailing cause of ill-
will, and that if such a visit as this had any effect at all on
Anglo-Soviet relations, it could only be to make them slightly
worse than before.

Even the newspapers have been unable to conceal the fact
that at least two of the four matches played led to much bad
feeling. At the Arsenal match, I am told by someone who was
there, a British and a Russian player came to blows and the
crowd booed the referee. The Glasgow match, someone else
informs me, was simply a free-for-all from the start. And then
there was the controversy, typical of our nationalistic age,
about the composition of the Arsenal team. Was it really an
all-England team, as claimed by the Russians, or merely a
league team, as claimed by the British? And did the Dynamos
end their tour abruptly in order to avoid playing an all-
England team? As usual, everyone answers these questions according to his political predilections. No doubt the controversy will continue to echo for years in the footnotes of history books. Meanwhile the result of the Dynamos' tour, in so

[1] The Moscow Dynamos, a Russian football team, toured Britain in the
autumn of 1945, playing against leading clubs.

far as it has had any result, will have been to create fresh animosity on both sides.

And how could it be otherwise? I am always amazed when I hear people saying that sport creates goodwill between the nations, and that if only the common peoples of the world could meet one another at football or cricket, they would have no inclination to meet on the battlefield. Even if one didn't know from concrete examples (the 1936 Olympic Games, for instance) that international sporting contests lead to orgies of hatred, one could deduce it from general principles.

Nearly all the sports practised nowadays are competitive. You play to win, and the game has little meaning unless you do your utmost to win. On the village green, where you pick up sides and no feeling of local patriotism is involved, it is possible to play simply for the fun and exercise: but as soon as the question of prestige arises, as soon as you feel that you and some larger unit will be disgraced if you lose, the most savage combative instincts are aroused. Anyone who has played even in a school football match knows this. At the international level, sport is frankly mimic warfare. But the significant thing is not the behavior of the players but the attitude of the spectators: and, behind the spectators, of the nations who work themselves into furies over these absurd contests, and seriously believe—at any rate for short periods— that running, jumping and kicking a ball are tests of national virtue.

Even a leisurely game like cricket, demanding grace rather than strength, can cause much ill-will, as we saw in the controversy over body-line bowling and over the rough tactics of the Australian team that visited England in 1921. Football, a game in which everyone gets hurt and every nation has its own style of play which seems unfair to foreigners, is far

worse. Worst of all is boxing. One of the most horrible sights
in the world is a fight between white and colored boxers before a mixed audience. But a boxing audience is always disgusting, and the behavior of the women, in particular, is such
that the Army, I believe, does not allow them to attend its
contests. At any rate, two or three years ago, when Home
Guards and regular troops were holding a boxing tournament,
I was placed on guard at the door of the hall, with orders to
keep the women out.

In England, the obsession with sport is bad enough, but
even fiercer passions are aroused in young countries where
games-playing and nationalism are both recent developments.
In countries like India or Burma, it is necessary at football
matches to have strong cordons of police to keep the crowd
from invading the field. In Burma, I have seen the supporters
of one side break through the police and disable the goal-
keeper of the opposing side at a critical moment. The first big
football match that was played in Spain, about fifteen years
ago, led to an uncontrollable riot. As soon as strong feelings
of rivalry are aroused, the notion of playing the game according to the rules always vanishes. People want to see one side on
top and the other side humiliated and they forget that victory
gained through cheating or through the intervention of the
crowd is meaningless. Even when the spectators don't inter-
vene physically they try to influence the game by cheering
their own side and "rattling" opposing players with boos and
insults. Serious sport has nothing to do with fair play. It is
bound up with hatred, jealousy, boastfulness, disregard of all
rules and sadistic pleasure in witnessing violence: in other
words it is war minus the shooting.

Instead of blah-blahing about the clean, healthy rivalry of
the football field and the great part played by the Olympic
Games in bringing the nations together, it is more useful to

inquire how and why this modern cult of sport arose. Most of
the games we now play are of ancient origin, but sport does
not seem to have been taken very seriously between Roman
times and the nineteenth century. Even in the English public
schools the games cult did not start till the later part of the
last century. Dr. Arnold, generally regarded as the founder of
the modern public school, looked on games as simply a waste
of time. Then, chiefly in England and the United States,
games were built up into a heavily financed activity, capable
of attracting vast crowds and rousing savage passions, and the
infection spread from country to country. It is the most violently combative sports, football and boxing, that have spread
the widest. There cannot be much doubt that the whole thing
is bound up with the rise of nationalism—that is, with the
lunatic modern habit of identifying oneself with large power
units and seeing everything in terms of competitive prestige.
Also, organized games are more likely to flourish in urban
communities where the average human being lives a sedentary
or at least a confined life, and does not get much opportunity
for creative labor. In a rustic community a boy or young man
works off a good deal of his surplus energy by walking, swimming, snowballing, climbing trees, riding horses, and by
various sports involving cruelty to animals, such as fishing,
cock-fighting and ferreting for rats. In a big town one must
indulge in group activities if one wants an outlet for one's
physical strength or for one's sadistic impulses. Games are
taken seriously in London and New York, and they were taken
seriously in Rome and Byzantium; in the Middle Ages they
were played, and probably played with much physical brutality, but they were not mixed up with politics nor a cause
of group hatreds.

If you wanted to add to the vast fund of ill-will existing in
the world at this moment, you could hardly do it better than

by a series of football matches between Jews and Arabs, Germans and Czechs, Indians and British, Russians and Poles, and Italians and Yugoslavs, each match to be watched by a mixed audience of 100,000 spectators. I do not, of course, suggest that sport is one of the main causes of international rivalry; big-scale sport is itself, I think, merely another effect of the causes that have produced nationalism. Still, you do make things worse by sending forth a team of eleven men, labelled as national champions, to do battle against some rival team, and allowing it to be felt on all sides that whichever nation is defeated will "lose face."

I hope, therefore, that we shan't follow up the visit of the Dynamos by sending a British team to the U.S.S.R. If we must do so, then let us send a second-rate team which is sure to be beaten and cannot be claimed to represent Britain as a whole. There are quite enough real causes of trouble already, and we need not add to them by encouraging young men to kick each other on the shins amid the roars of infuriated spectators.

Decline of the English Murder

IT IS SUNDAY AFTERNOON, PREFERABLY BEFORE THE WAR. THE wife is already asleep in the armchair, and the children have been sent out for a nice long walk. You put your feet up on the sofa, settle your spectacles on your nose, and open the *News of the World*. Roast beef and Yorkshire, or roast pork and apple sauce, followed up by suet pudding and driven home, as it were, by a cup of mahogany-brown tea, have put you in just the right mood. Your pipe is drawing sweetly, the sofa cushions are soft underneath you, the fire is well alight, the air is warm and stagnant. In these blissful circumstances, what is it that you want to read about?

Naturally, about a murder. But what kind of murder? If one examines the murders which have given the greatest amount of pleasure to the British public, the murders whose story is known in its general outline to almost everyone and which have been made into novels and re-hashed over and over again by the Sunday papers, one finds a fairly strong family resemblance running through the greater number of them. Our great period in murder, our Elizabethan period, so to speak, seems to have been between roughly 1850 and 1925, and the murderers whose reputation has stood the test of time are the following: Dr. Palmer of Rugely, Jack the Ripper, Neill Cream, Mrs. Maybrick, Dr. Crippen, Seddon, Joseph Smith, Armstrong and Bywaters and Thompson. In addition, in 1919 or thereabouts, there was another very celebrated case which fits into the general pattern but which I had better not mention by name, because the accused man was acquitted.

Of the above-mentioned nine cases, at least four have had successful novels based on them, one has been made into a popular melodrama, and the amount of literature surrounding them, in the form of newspaper write-ups, criminological treatises and reminiscences by lawyers and police officers, would make a considerable library. It is difficult to believe that any recent English crime will be remembered so long and so intimately, and not only because the violence of external events has made murder seem unimportant, but because the prevalent type of crime seems to be changing. The principal *cause célèbre* of the war years was the so-called Cleft Chin Murder, which has now been written up in a popular booklet [1] the verbatim account of the trial was published some time last year by Messrs. Jarrolds with an introduction by Mr. Bechhofer Roberts. Before returning to this pitiful and sordid case, which is only interesting from a sociological and perhaps a legal point of view, let me try to define what it is that the readers of Sunday papers mean when they say fretfully that "you never seem to get a good murder nowadays."

In considering the nine murders I named above, one can start by excluding the Jack the Ripper case, which is in a class by itself. Of the other eight, six were poisoning cases, and eight of the ten criminals belonged to the middle class. In one way or another, sex was a powerful motive in all but two cases, and in at least four cases respectability—the desire to gain a secure position in life, or not to forfeit one's social position by some scandal such as a divorce—was one of the main reasons for committing murder. In more than half the cases, the object

[1] *The Cleft Chin Murder,* by R. Alwyn Raymond, Claude Morris.

was to get hold of a certain known sum of money such as a
legacy or an insurance policy, but the amount involved was
nearly always small. In most of the cases the crime only came
to light slowly, as the result of careful investigations which
started off with the suspicions of neighbors or relatives; and in
nearly every case there was some dramatic coincidence, in
which the finger of Providence could be clearly seen, or one
of those episodes that no novelist would dare to make up,
such as Crippen's flight across the Atlantic with his mistress
dressed as a boy, or Joseph Smith playing "Nearer, my God,
to Thee" on the harmonium while one of his wives was drown-
ing in the next room. The background of all these crimes,
except Neill Cream's, was essentially domestic; of twelve vic-
tims, seven were either wife or husband of the murderer.

With all this in mind one can construct what would be,
from a *News of the World* reader's point of view, the "perfect"
murder. The murderer should be a little man of the professional class—a dentist or a solicitor, say—living an intensely
respectable life somewhere in the suburbs, and preferably in
a semi-detached house, which will allow the neighbors to hear
suspicious sounds through the wall. He should be either chair-
man of the local Conservative Party branch, or a leading Non-
conformist and strong Temperance advocate. He should go
astray through cherishing a guilty passion for his secretary or
the wife of a rival professional man, and should only bring
himself to the point of murder after long and terrible wrestles
with his conscience. Having decided on murder, he should
plan it all with the utmost cunning, and only slip up over
some tiny unforeseeable detail. The means chosen should, of
course, be poison. In the last analysis he should commit murder because this seems to him less disgraceful, and less damag-
ing to his career, than being detected in adultery. With this
kind of background, a crime can have dramatic and even tragic

qualities which make it memorable and excite pity for both victim and murderer. Most of the crimes mentioned above have a touch of this atmosphere, and in three cases, including the one I referred to but did not name, the story approximates to the one I have outlined.

Now compare the Cleft Chin Murder. There is no depth of feeling in it. It was almost chance that the two people concerned committed that particular murder, and it was only by good luck that they did not commit several others. The background was not domesticity, but the anonymous life of the dance-halls and the false values of the American film. The two culprits were an eighteen-year-old ex-waitress named Elizabeth Jones, and an American army deserter, posing as an officer, named Karl Hulten. They were only together for six days, and it seems doubtful whether until they were arrested, they even learned one another's true names. They met casually in a teashop, and that night went out for a ride in a stolen army truck. Jones described herself as a strip-tease artist, which was not strictly true (she had given one unsuccessful performance in this line), and declared that she wanted to do something dangerous, "like being a gun-moll." Hulten described himself as a big-time Chicago gangster, which was also untrue. They met a girl bicycling along the road, and to show how tough he was Hulten ran over her with his truck, after which the pair robbed her of the few shillings that were on her. On another occasion they knocked out a girl to whom they had offered a lift, took her coat and handbag and threw her into a river. Finally, in the most wanton way, they murdered a taxi-driver who happened to have £8 in his pocket. Soon afterwards they parted. Hulten was caught because he had foolishly kept the dead man's car, and Jones made spontaneous confessions to the police. In court each prisoner incriminated the other. In between crimes, both of them seem to have behaved with the utmost callousness: they spent the dead taxi-driver's £8 at the dog races.

Judging from her letters, the girl's case has a certain amount of psychological interest, but this murder probably captured the headlines because it provided distraction amid the doodle-bugs and the anxieties of the Battle of France. Jones and Hulten committed their murder to the tune of V-1, and were convicted to the tune of V-2. There was also considerable excitement because—as has become usual in England—the man was sentenced to death and the girl to imprisonment. According to Mr. Raymond, the reprieving of Jones caused widespread indignation and streams of telegrams to the Home Secretary; in her native town, "She should hang" was chalked on the walls beside pictures of a figure dangling from a gallows. Considering that only ten women have been hanged in Britain this century, and that the practice has gone out largely because of popular feeling against it, it is difficult not to feel that this clamor to hang an eighteen-year-old girl was due partly to the brutalizing effects of war. Indeed, the whole meaningless story, with its atmosphere of dance-halls, movie-palaces, cheap perfume, false names and stolen cars, belongs essentially to a war period.

Perhaps it is significant that the most talked-of English murder of recent years should have been committed by an American and an English girl who had become partly Americanized. But it is difficult to believe that this case will be so long remembered as the old domestic poisoning dramas, product of a stable society where the all-prevailing hypocrisy did at least ensure that crimes as serious as murder should have strong emotions behind them.

Some Thoughts
on the Common Toad

BEFORE THE SWALLOW, BEFORE THE DAFFODIL, AND NOT MUCH later than the snowdrop, the common toad salutes the coming of spring after his own fashion, which is to emerge from a hole in the ground, where he has lain buried since the previous autumn, and crawl as rapidly as possible towards the nearest suitable patch of water. Something—some kind of shudder in the earth, or perhaps merely a rise of a few degrees in the temperature—has told him that it is time to wake up: though a few toads appear to sleep the clock round and miss out a year from time to time—at any rate, I have more than once dug them up, alive and apparently well, in the middle of the summer.

At this period, after his long fast, the toad has a very spiritual look, like a strict Anglo-Catholic towards the end of Lent. His movements are languid but purposeful, his body is shrunken, and by contrast his eyes look abnormally large. This allows one to notice, what one might not at another time, that a toad has about the most beautiful eye of any living creature. It is like gold, or more exactly it is like the golden-colored semi-precious stone which one sometimes sees in signet rings, and which I think is called a chrysoberyl.

For a few days after getting into the water the toad concentrates on building up his strength by eating small insects.

Presently he has swollen to his normal size again, and then
he goes through a phase of intense sexiness. All he knows, at
least if he is a male toad, is that he wants to get his arms round
something, and if you offer him a stick, or even your finger, he
will cling to it with surprising strength and take a long time
to discover that it is not a female toad. Frequently one comes
upon shapeless masses of ten or twenty toads rolling over and
over in the water, one clinging to another without distinction
of sex. By degrees, however, they sort themselves out into cou-
ples, with the male duly sitting on the female's back. You can
now distinguish males from females, because the male is
smaller, darker and sits on top, with his arms tightly clasped
round the female's neck. After a day or two the spawn is laid
in long strings which wind themselves in and out of the reeds
and soon become invisible. A few more weeks, and the water
is alive with masses of tiny tadpoles which rapidly grow larger,
sprout hind-legs, then fore-legs, then shed their tails: and
finally, about the middle of the summer, the new generation
of toads, smaller than one's thumb-nail but perfect in every
particular, crawl out of the water to begin the game anew.

I mention the spawning of the toads because it is one of
the phenomena of spring which most deeply appeal to me,
and because the toad, unlike the skylark and the primrose, has
never had much of a boost from the poets. But I am aware that
many people do not like reptiles or amphibians, and I am not
suggesting that in order to enjoy the spring you have to take
an interest in toads. There are also the crocus, the missel
thrush, the cuckoo, the blackthorn, etc. The point is that the
pleasures of spring are available to everybody, and cost nothing. Even in the most sordid street the coming of spring will
register itself by some sign or other, if it is only a brighter
blue between the chimney pots or the vivid green of an elder

sprouting on a blitzed site. Indeed it is remarkable how Nature goes on existing unofficially, as it were, in the very heart of London. I have seen a kestrel flying over the Deptford gasworks, and I have heard a first-rate performance by a black bird in the Euston Road. There must be some hundreds of thousands, if not millions, of birds living inside the four-mile radius, and it is rather a pleasing thought that none of them pays a halfpenny of rent.

As for spring, not even the narrow and gloomy streets round the Bank of England are quite able to exclude it. It comes seeping in everywhere, like one of those new poison gases which pass through all filters. The spring is commonly referred to as "a miracle," and during the past five or six years this worn-out figure of speech has taken on a new lease of life. After the sort of winters we have had to endure recently, the spring does seem miraculous, because it has become gradually harder and harder to believe that it is actually going to happen. Every February since 1940 I have found myself thinking that this time winter is going to be permanent. But Persephone, like the toads, always rises from the dead at about the same moment. Suddenly, towards the end of March, the miracle happens and the decaying slum in which I live is transfigured. Down in the square the sooty privets have turned bright green, the leaves are thickening on the chestnut trees, the daffodils are out, the wallflowers are budding, the policeman's tunic looks positively a pleasant shade of blue, the fishmonger greets his customers with a smile, and even the sparrows are quite a different color, having felt the balminess of the air and nerved themselves to take a bath, their first since last September.

Is it wicked to take a pleasure in spring, and other seasonal changes? To put it more precisely, is it politically reprehensi-

ble, while we are all groaning, under the shackles of the capitalist system, to point out that life is frequently more worth
living because of a blackbird's song, a yellow elm tree in
October, or some other natural phenomenon which does not
cost money and does not have what the editors of the Left-
wing newspapers call a class angle? There is no doubt that
many people think so. I know by experience that a favorable
reference to "Nature" in one of my articles is liable to bring
me abusive letters, and though the key-word in these letters is
usually "sentimental," two ideas seem to be mixed up in them.
One is that any pleasure in the actual process of life encour-
ages a sort of political quietism. People, so the thought runs,
ought to be discontented, and it is our job to multiply our
wants and not simply to increase our enjoyment of the things
we have already. The other idea is that this is the age of
machines and that to dislike the machine, or even to want to
limit its domination, is backward-looking, reactionary, and
slightly ridiculous. This is often backed up by the statement
that a love of Nature is a foible of urbanized people who have
no notion what Nature is really like. Those who really have to
deal with the soil, so it is argued, do not love the soil, and do
not take the faintest interest in birds or flowers, except from a
strictly utilitarian point of view. To love the country one
must live in the town, merely taking an occasional week-end
ramble at the warmer times of year.

This last idea is demonstrably false. Medieval literature,
for instance, including the popular ballads, is full of an
almost Georgian enthusiasm for Nature, and the art of agri-
cultural peoples such as the Chinese and Japanese centres
always round trees, birds, flowers, rivers, mountains. The other
idea seems to me to be wrong in a subtler way. Certainly we
ought to be discontented, we ought not simply to find out
ways of making the best of a bad job, and yet if we kill all

pleasure in the actual process of life, what sort of future are we preparing for ourselves? If a man cannot enjoy the return of spring, why should he be happy in a labor-saving Utopia? What will he do with the leisure that the machine will give him? I have always suspected that if our economic and political problems are ever really solved, life will become simpler instead of more complex, and that the sort of pleasure one gets from finding the first primrose will loom larger than the sort of pleasure one gets from eating an ice to the tune of a Wurlitzer. I think that by retaining one's childhood love of such things as trees, fishes, butterflies and—to return to my first instance—toads, one makes a peaceful and decent future a little more probable, and that by preaching the doctrine that nothing is to be admired except steel and concrete, one merely makes it a little surer that human beings will have no outlet for their surplus energy except in hatred and leader-worship.

At any rate, spring is here, even in London, N.1, and they can't stop you enjoying it. This is a satisfying reflection. How many a time have I stood watching the toads mating, or a pair of hares having a boxing match in the young corn, and thought of all the important persons who would stop me enjoying this if they could. But luckily they can't. So long as you are not actually ill, hungry, frightened or immured in a prison or a holiday camp, spring is still spring. The atom bombs are piling up in the factories, the police are prowling through the cities, the lies are streaming from the loudspeakers, but the earth is still going round the sun, and neither the dictators nor the bureaucrats, deeply as they disapprove of the process, are able to prevent it.

A Good Word
for the Vicar of Bray

SOME YEARS AGO A FRIEND TOOK ME TO THE LITTLE BERKSHIRE church of which the celebrated Vicar of Bray was once the incumbent. (Actually it is a few miles from Bray, but perhaps at that time the two livings were one.) In the churchyard there stands a magnificent yew tree which, according to a notice at its foot, was planted by no less a person than the Vicar of Bray himself. And it struck me at the time as curious that such a man should have left such a relic behind him.

The Vicar of Bray, though he was well equipped to be a leader-writer on *The Times*, could hardly be described as an admirable character. Yet, after this lapse of time, all that is left of him is a comic song [1] and a beautiful tree, which has rested the eyes of generation after generation and must surely have outweighed any bad effects which he produced by his political quislingism.

Thibaw, the last King of Burma, was also far from being a good man. He was a drunkard, he had five hundred wives— he seems to have kept them chiefly for show, however—and when he came to the throne his first act was to decapitate seventy or eighty of his brothers. Yet he did posterity a good

[1] An anonymous song dating from the 18th Century. The subject is a parson who boasts that he has accommodated himself to the religious views of the reigns of Charles, James, William, Anne, and George and that, whatever king may reign, he will remain Vicar of Bray.

turn by planting the dusty streets of Mandalay with tamarind trees which cast a pleasant shade until the Japanese incendiary bombs burned them down in 1942.

The poet, James Shirley, seems to have generalized too freely when he said that "Only the actions of the just Smell sweet and blossom in their dust." Sometimes the actions of the unjust make quite a good showing after the appropriate lapse of time. When I saw the Vicar of Bray's yew tree it reminded me of something, and afterwards I got hold of a book of selections from the writings of John Aubrey and re-read a pastoral poem which must have been written some time in the first half of the seventeenth century, and which was inspired by a certain Mrs. Overall.

Mrs. Overall was the wife of a Dean and was extensively unfaithful to him. According to Aubrey she "could scarcely denie any one," and she had "the loveliest Eies that were ever seen, but wondrous wanton." The poem (the "shepherd swaine" seems to have been somebody called Sir John Selby) starts off:

> Downe lay the Shepherd Swaine
> So sober and demure
> Wishing for his wench againe
> So bonny and so pure
> With his head on hillock lowe
> And his arms akimboe
> And all was for the losse of his
> Hye nonny nonny noe. . . .
> Sweet she was, as kind a love
> As ever fetter'd Swaine;
> Never such a daynty one
> Shall man enjoy again.
> Sett a thousand on a rowe
> I forbid that any showe
> Ever the like of her
> Hye nonny nonny noe.

As the poem proceeds through another six verses, the refrain "hye nonny nonny noe" takes on an unmistakably obscene meaning, but it ends with the exquisite stanza:

> But gone she is the prettiest lasse
> That ever trod on plaine.
> What ever hath betide of her
> Blame not the Shepherd Swaine.
> For why? She was her owne Foe,
> And gave herself the overthrowe
> By being so franke of her
> Hye nonny nonny noe.

Mrs. Overall was no more an exemplary character than the Vicar of Bray, though a more attractive one. Yet in the end all that remains of her is a poem which still gives pleasure to many people, though for some reason it never gets into the anthologies. The suffering which she presumably caused, and the misery and futility in which her own life must have ended, have been transformed into a sort of lingering fragrance like the smell of tobacco-plants on a summer evening.

But to come back to trees. The planting of a tree, especially one of the long-living hardwood trees, is a gift which you can make to posterity at almost no cost and with almost no trouble, and if the tree takes root it will far outlive the visible effect of any of your other actions, good or evil. A year or two ago I wrote a few paragraphs in *Tribune* about some sixpenny rambler roses from Woolworth's which I had planted before the war This brought me an indignant letter from a reader who said that roses are bourgeois, but I still think that my sixpence was better spent than if it had gone on cigarettes or even on one of the excellent Fabian Research Pamphlets.

Recently, I spent a day at the cottage where I used to live, and noted with a pleased surprise—to be exact, it was a feeling of having done good unconsciously—the progress of the things

I had planted nearly ten years ago. I think it is worth recording what some of them cost, just to show what you can do
with a few shillings if you invest them in something that
grows.

First of all there were the two ramblers from Woolworth's,
and three polyantha roses, all at sixpence each. Then there
were two bush roses which were part of a job lot from a nursery garden. This job lot consisted of six fruit trees, three rose
bushes and two gooseberry bushes, all for ten shillings. One
of the fruit trees and one of the rose bushes died but the rest
are all flourishing. The sum total is five fruit trees, seven roses
and two gooseberry bushes, all for twelve and sixpence. These
plants have not entailed much work, and have had nothing
spent on them beyond the original amount. They never even
received any manure, except what I occasionally collected in
a bucket when one of the farm horses happened to have halted
outside the gate.

Between them, in nine years, those seven rose bushes will
have given what would add up to a hundred or a hundred and
fifty months of bloom. The fruit trees, which were mere sap-
lings when I put them in, are now just about getting in their
stride. Last week one of them, a plum, was a mass of blossom,
and the apples looked as if they were going to do fairly well.
What had originally been the weakling of the family, a Cox's
Orange Pippin—it would hardly have been included in the
job lot if it had been a good plant—had grown into a sturdy
tree with plenty of fruit spurs on it. I maintain that it was
a public-spirited action to plant that Cox, for these trees do
not fruit quickly and I did not expect to stay there long. I
never had an apple off it myself, but it looks as if someone
else will have quite a lot. By their fruits ye shall know them,
and the Cox's Orange Pippin is a good fruit to be known by.
Yet I did not plant it with the conscious intention of doing

anybody a good turn. I just saw the job lot going cheap and
stuck the things into the ground without much preparation.

A thing which I regret, and which I will try to remedy some
time, is that I have never in my life planted a walnut. Nobody
does plant them nowadays—when you see a walnut it is almost
invariably an old tree. If you plant a walnut you are planting
it for your grandchildren, and who cares a damn for his grandchildren? Nor does anybody plant a quince, a mulberry or a
medlar. But these are garden trees which you can only be
expected to plant if you have a patch of ground of your own.
On the other hand, in any hedge or in any piece of waste
ground you happen to be walking through, you can do something to remedy the appalling massacre of trees, especially
oaks, ashes, elms and beeches, which has happened during the
war years.

Even an apple tree is liable to live for about 100 years, so
that the Cox I planted in 1936 may still be bearing fruit well
into the twenty-first century. An oak or a beech may live for
hundreds of years and be a pleasure to thousands or tens of
thousands of people before it is finally sawn up into timber.
I am not suggesting that one can discharge all one's obliga-
tions towards society by means of a private re-afforestation
scheme. Still, it might not be a bad idea, every time you commit an anti-social act, to make a note of it in your diary, and
then, at the appropriate season, push an acorn into the ground.

And, if even one in twenty of them came to maturity, you
might do quite a lot of harm in your lifetime, and still, like
the Vicar of Bray, end up as a public benefactor after all.

Confessions of a Book Reviewer

IN A COLD BUT STUFFY BED-SITTING ROOM LITTERED WITH CIGA-rette ends and half-empty cups of tea, a man in a moth-eaten dressing gown sits at a rickety table, trying to find room for his typewriter among the piles of dusty papers that surround it. He cannot throw the papers away because the wastepaper basket is already overflowing, and besides, somewhere among the unanswered letters and unpaid bills it is possible that there is a cheque for two guineas which he is nearly certain he forgot to pay into the bank. There are also letters with addresses which ought to be entered in his address book. He has lost his address book, and the thought of looking for it, or indeed of looking for anything, afflicts him with acute suicidal impulses.

He is a man of thirty-five, but looks fifty. He is bald, has varicose veins and wears spectacles, or would wear them if his only pair were not chronically lost. If things are normal with him he will be suffering from malnutrition, but if he has recently had a lucky streak he will be suffering from a hangover. At present it is half-past eleven in the morning, and according to his schedule he should have started work two hours ago; but even if he had made any serious effort to start he would have been frustrated by the almost continuous ringing of the telephone bell, the yells of the baby, the rattle of an electric drill out in the street, and the heavy boots of his creditors clumping up and down the stairs. The most recent interruption was the arrival of the second post, which brought him two circulars and an income tax demand printed in red.

Needless to say this person is a writer. He might be a poet, a novelist, or a writer of film scripts or radio features, for all literary people are very much alike, but let us say that he is a book reviewer. Half hidden among the pile of papers is a bulky parcel containing five volumes which his editor has sent with a note suggesting that they "ought to go well together." They arrived four days ago, but for forty-eight hours the reviewer was prevented by moral paralysis from opening the parcel. Yesterday in a resolute moment he ripped the string off it and found the five volumes to be *Palestine at the Cross Roads, Scientific Dairy Farming, A Short History of European Democracy* (this one is 680 pages and weighs four pounds), *Tribal Customs in Portuguese East Africa,* and a novel *It's Nicer Lying Down,* probably included by mistake. His review —800 words, say—has got to be "in" by mid-day tomorrow.

Three of these books deal with subjects of which he is so ignorant that he will have to read at least fifty pages if he is to avoid making some howler which will betray him not merely to the author (who of course knows all about the habits of book reviewers), but even to the general reader. By four in the afternoon he will have taken the books out of their wrapping paper but will still be suffering from a nervous inability to open them. The prospect of having to read them, and even the smell of the paper, affects him like the prospect of eating cold ground-rice pudding flavored with castor oil. And yet curiously enough his copy will get to the office in time. Somehow it always does get there in time. At about nine P.M. his mind will grow relatively clear, and until the small hours he will sit in a room which grows colder and colder, while the cigarette smoke grows thicker and thicker, skipping expertly through one book after another and laying each down with the final comment, "God, what tripe!" In the morning, blear-eyed, surly and unshaven, he will gaze for an hour or two at a blank sheet of paper until the menacing finger of the clock frightens him into action. Then suddenly he will snap into it. All the stale old phrases—"a book that no one should miss," "something memorable on every page," "of special value are the chapters dealing with, etc., etc."— will jump into their places like iron filings obeying the magnet, and the review will end up at exactly the right length and with just about three minutes to go. Meanwhile another wad of ill-assorted unappetizing books will have arrived by post. So it goes on. And yet with what high hopes this downtrodden, nerve-racked creature started his career, only a few years ago.

Do I seem to exaggerate? I ask any regular reviewer—anyone who reviews, say, a minimum of 100 books a year—whether he can deny in honesty that his habits and character are such as I have described. Every writer, in any case, is rather that kind of person, but the prolonged, indiscriminate reviewing of books is a quite exceptionally thankless, irritating and exhausting job. It not only involves praising trash—though it does involve that, as I will show in a moment—but constantly *inventing* reactions towards books about which one has no spontaneous feelings whatever. The reviewer, jaded though he may be, is professionally interested in books, and out of the thousands that appear annually, there are probably fifty or a hundred that he would enjoy writing about. If he is a topnotcher in his profession he may get hold of ten or twenty of them: more probably he gets hold of two or three. The rest of his work, however conscientious he may be in praising or damning, is in essence humbug. He is pouring his immortal spirit down the drain, half a pint at a time.

The great majority of reviews give an inadequate or misleading account of the book that is dealt with. Since the war publishers have been less able than before to twist the tails of literary editors and evoke a paean of praise for every book that they produce, but on the other hand the standard of reviewing has gone down owing to lack of space and other inconveniences. Seeing the results, people sometimes suggest that the solution lies in getting book-reviewing out of the hands of hacks. Books on specialized subjects ought to be dealt with by experts, and on the other hand a good deal of reviewing, especially of novels, might well be done by amateurs. Nearly every book is capable of arousing passionate feeling, if it is only a passionate dislike, in some or other reader, whose ideas about it would surely be worth more than those of a bored professional. But, unfortunately as every editor knows, that kind of thing is very difficult to organize. In practice the editor always finds himself reverting to his team of hacks—his "regulars," as he calls them.

None of this is remediable so long as it is taken for granted that every book deserves to be reviewed. It is almost impossible to mention books in bulk without grossly over-praising the great majority of them. Until one has some kind of professional relationship with books one does not discover how bad the majority of them are. In much more than nine cases out of ten the only objectively truthful criticism would be, "This book is worthless," while the truth about the reviewer's own reaction would probably be: "This book does not interest me in any way, and I would not write about it unless I were paid to." But the public will not pay to read that kind of thing. Why should they? They want some kind of guide to the books they are asked to read, and they want some kind of evaluation. But as soon as values are mentioned, standards collapse. For if one says—and nearly every reviewer says this kind of thing at least once a week—that *King Lear* is a good play and *The*

Four Just Men is a good thriller, what meaning is there in the word "good"?

The best practice, it has always seemed to me, would be simply to ignore the great majority of books and to give very long reviews—1,000 words is a bare minimum—to the few that seem to matter. Short notes of a line or two on forthcoming books can be useful, but the usual middle-length review of about 600 words is bound to be worthless even if the reviewer genuinely wants to write it. Normally he doesn't want to write it, and the week-in, week-out production of snippets soon reduces him to the crushed figure in a dressing gown whom I described at the beginning of this article. However, everyone in this world has someone else whom he can look down on, and I must say, from experience of both trades, that the book reviewer is better off than the film critic, who cannot even do his work at home, but has to attend trade shows at eleven in the morning and, with one or two notable exceptions, is expected to sell his honor for a glass of inferior sherry.

Books vs. Cigarettes

A COUPLE OF YEARS AGO A FRIEND OF MINE, A NEWSPAPER EDITOR, was fire-watching with some factory workers. They fell to talking about his newspaper, which most of them read and approved of, but when he asked them what they thought of the literary section, the answer he got was: "You don't suppose we read that stuff, do you? Why, half the time you're talking about books that cost twelve and sixpence! Chaps like us couldn't spend twelve and sixpence on a book." These, he said, were men who thought nothing of spending several pounds on a day trip to Blackpool.

This idea that the buying, or even the reading, of books is an expensive hobby and beyond the reach of the average person is so widespread that it deserves some detailed examination. Exactly what reading costs, reckoned in terms of pence per hour, is difficult to estimate, but I have made a start by inventorying my own books and adding up their total price. After allowing for various other expenses, I can make a fairly good guess at my expenditure over the last fifteen years.

The books that I have counted and priced are the ones I have here, in my flat. I have about an equal number stored in another place, so that I shall double the final figure in order to arrive at the complete amount. I have not counted oddments such as proof copies, defaced volumes, cheap paper-

covered editions, pamphlets, or magazines, unless bound up
into book form. Nor have I counted the kind of junky books
—old school textbooks and so forth—that accumulate in the
bottoms of cupboards. I have counted only those books which
I have acquired voluntarily, or else would have acquired
voluntarily, and which I intend to keep. In this category I
find that I have 442 books, acquired in the following ways:

Bought (mostly second-hand)	251
Given to me or bought with book tokens	33
Review copies and complimentary copies	143
Borrowed and not returned	10
Temporarily on loan	5
	——
Total	442

Now as to the method of pricing. Those books that I have
bought I have listed at their full price, as closely as I can
determine it. I have also listed at their full price the books
that have been given to me, and those that I have temporarily
borrowed, or borrowed and kept. This is because book-giving,
book-borrowing and book-stealing more or less even out. I
possess books that do not strictly speaking belong to me, but
many other people also have books of mine: so that the books
I have not paid for can be taken as balancing others which
I have paid for but no longer possess. On the other hand I
have listed the review and complimentary copies at half-price.
That is about what I would have paid for them second-hand,
and they are mostly books that I would only have bought
second-hand, if at all. For the prices I have sometimes had to
rely on guesswork, but my figures will not be far out. The costs
were as follows:

	£	s.	d.
Bought	36	9	0
Gifts	10	10	6
Review copies, etc.	25	11	9
Borrowed and not returned	4	16	9
On loan	3	10	6
Shelves	2	0	0
Total	82	17	6

Adding the other batch of books that I have elsewhere, it seems that I possess, altogether, nearly 900 books, at a cost of £165 15s. This is the accumulation of about fifteen years—actually more, since some of these books date from my childhood: but call it fifteen years. This works out at £11 1s. a year, but there are other charges that must be added in order to estimate my full reading expenses. The biggest will be for newspapers and periodicals, and for this I think £8 a year would be a reasonable figure. Eight pounds a year covers the cost of two daily papers, one evening paper, two Sunday papers, one weekly review and one or two monthly magazines. This brings the figure up to £19 1s. but to arrive at the grand total one has to make a guess. Obviously one often spends money on books without afterwards having anything to show for it. There are library subscriptions, and there are also the books, chiefly Penguins and other cheap editions, which one buys and then loses or throws away. However, on the basis of my other figures, it looks as though £6 a year would be quite enough to add for expenditure of this kind. So my total reading expenses over the past fifteen years have been in the neighborhood of £25 a year.

Twenty-five pounds a year sounds quite a lot until you begin to measure it against other kinds of expenditure. It is nearly 9s. 9d. a week, and at present 9s. 9d. is the equivalent of about 83 cigarettes (Players): even before the war it would have bought you less than 200 cigarettes. With prices as they now are, I am spending far more on tobacco than I do on books. I smoke six ounces a week, at half-a-crown an ounce, making nearly £40 a year. Even before the war when the same tobacco cost 8d. an ounce, I was spending over £10 a year on it: and if I also average a pint of beer a day, at sixpence, these two items together will have cost me close on £20 a year. This was probably not much above the national average. In 1938 the people of England spent nearly £10 per head per annum on alcohol and tobacco: however, 20 per cent. of the population were children under fifteen and another 40 per cent. were women, so that the average smoker and drinker must have been spending much more than £10. In 1944, the annual expenditure per head on these items was no less than £23. Allow for the women and children as before, and £40 is a reasonable individual figure. Forty pounds a year would just about pay for a packet of Woodbines every day and half a pint of mild six days a week—not a magnificent allowance. Of course, all prices are now inflated, including the price of books: still, it looks as though the cost of reading, even if you buy books instead of borrowing them and take in a fairly large number of periodicals, does not amount to more than the combined cost of smoking and drinking.

It is difficult to establish any relationship between the price of books and the value one gets out of them. "Books" includes novels, poetry, textbooks, works of reference, sociological treatises and much else, and length and price do not correspond to one another, especially if one habitually buys books second-hand. You may spend ten shillings on a poem of 500 lines, and you may spend sixpence on a dictionary which you consult at odd moments over a period of twenty years. There

are books that one reads over and over again, books that become part of the furniture of one's mind and alter one's
whole attitude to life, books that one dips into but never
reads through, books that one reads at a single sitting and
forgets a week later: and the cost, in terms of money, may be
the same in each case. But if one regards reading simply as a
recreation, like going to the pictures, then it is possible to
make a rough estimate of what it costs. If you read nothing
but novels and "light" literature, and bought every book that
you read, you would be spending—allowing eight shillings as
the price of a book, and four hours as the time spent in reading
it—two shillings an hour. This is about what it costs to sit in
one of the more expensive seats in the cinema. If you concen-
trated on more serious books, and still bought everything that
you read, your expenses would be about the same. The books
would cost more, but they would take longer to read. In either
case you would still possess the books after you had read them,
and they would be saleable at about a third of their purchase
price. If you bought only second-hand books, your reading
expenses would, of course, be much less: perhaps sixpence an
hour would be a fair estimate. And on the other hand if you
don't buy books, but merely borrow them from the lending
library, reading costs you round about a halfpenny an hour:
if you borrow them from the public library, it costs you next
door to nothing.

I have said enough to show that reading is one of the
cheaper recreations: after listening to the radio probably *the*
cheapest. Meanwhile, what is the actual amount that the
British public spends on books? I cannot discover any figures,
though no doubt they exist. But I do know that before the
war this country was publishing annually about 15,000 books,
which included reprints and schoolbooks. If as many as
10,000 copies of each book were sold—and even allowing for

the schoolbooks, this is probably a high estimate—the average person was only buying, directly or indirectly, about three books a year. These three books taken together might cost £1, or probably less.

These figures are guesswork, and I should be interested if someone would correct them for me. But if my estimate is anywhere near right, it is not a proud record for a country which is nearly 100 per cent. literate and where the ordinary man spends more on cigarettes than an Indian peasant has for his whole livelihood. And if our book-consumption remains as low as it has been, at least let us admit that it is because reading is a less exciting pastime than going to the dogs, the pictures or the pub, and not because books, whether bought or borrowed, are too expensive.

Good Bad Books

NOT LONG AGO A PUBLISHER COMMISSIONED ME TO WRITE AN introduction for a reprint of a novel by Leonard Merrick. This publishing house, it appears, is going to re-issue a long series of minor and partly-forgotten novels of the twentieth century. It is a valuable service in these bookless days, and I rather envy the person whose job it will be to scout round the threepenny boxes hunting down copies of his boyhood favorites.

A type of book which we hardly seem to produce in these days, but which flowered with great richness in the late nineteenth and early twentieth centuries, is what Chesterton called the "good bad book": that is, the kind of book that has no literary pretentions but which remains readable when more serious productions have perished. Obviously outstanding books in this line are *Raffles* and the *Sherlock Holmes* stories, which have kept their place when innumerable "problem novels," "human documents" and "terrible indictments" of this or that have fallen into deserved oblivion. (Who has worn better, Conan Doyle or Meredith?) Almost in the same class as these I put R. Austin Freeman's earlier stories—*The Singing Bone, The Eye of Osiris* and others—Ernest Bramah's *Max Carrados*, and, dropping the standard a bit, Guy Boothby's Tibetan thriller, *Dr. Nikola*, a sort of schoolboy version of Huc's *Travels in Tartary*, which would probably make a real visit to Central Asia seem a dismal anti-climax.

But apart from thrillers, there were the minor humorous writers of the period. For example, Pett Ridge—but I admit his full-length books no longer seem readable—E. Nesbit (*The Treasure Seekers*), George Birmingham, who was good so long as he kept off politics, the pornographic Binstead ("Pitcher" of the *Pink 'Un*), and, if American books are included, Booth Tarkington's Penrod stories. A cut above most of these was Barrie Pain. Some of Pain's humorous writings are, I suppose, still in print, but to anyone who comes across it I recommend what must now be a very rare book—*The Octave of Claudius*, a brilliant exercise in the macabre. Somewhat later in time there was Peter Blundell, who wrote in the W. W. Jacobs vein about Far Eastern seaport towns, and who seems to be rather unaccountably forgotten, in spite of having been praised in print by H. G. Wells.

However, all the books I have been speaking of are frankly "escape" literature. They form pleasant patches in one's memory, quiet corners where the mind can browse at odd moments, but they hardly pretend to have anything to do with real life. There is another kind of good bad book which is more seriously intended, and which tells us, I think, something about the nature of the novel and the reasons for its present decadence. During the last fifty years there has been a whole series of writers—some of them are still writing—whom it is quite impossible to call "good" by any strictly literary standard, but who are natural novelists and who seem to attain sincerity partly because they are not inhibited by good taste. In this class I put Leonard Merrick himself, W. L. George, J. D. Beresford, Ernest Raymond, May Sinclair, and—at a lower level than the others but still essentially similar—A. S. M. Hutchinson.

Most of these have been prolific writers, and their output has naturally varied in quality. I am thinking in each case of

one or two outstanding books: for example, Merrick's *Cynthia,*
J. D. Beresford's *A Candidate for Truth,* W. L. George's
Caliban, May Sinclair's *The Combined Maze,* and Ernest
Raymond's *We, the Accused.* In each of these books the author
has been able to identify himself with his imagined characters,
to feel with them and invite sympathy on their behalf, with a
kind of abandonment that cleverer people would find it difficult to achieve. They bring out the fact that intellectual
refinement can be a disadvantage to a storyteller, as it would
be to a music-hall comedian.

Take for example, Ernest Raymond's *We, the Accused*—a
peculiarly sordid and convincing murder story, probably
based on the Crippen case. I think it gains a great deal from
the fact that the author only partly grasps the pathetic vulgarity of the people he is writing about, and therefore does
not despise them. Perhaps it even—like Theodore Dreiser's
An American Tragedy—gains something from the clumsy long-
winded manner in which it is written; detail is piled on detail,
with almost no attempt at selection, and in the process an effect of terrible, grinding cruelty is slowly built up. So also with
A Candidate for Truth. Here there is not the same clumsiness,
but there is the same ability to take seriously the problems of
commonplace people. So also with *Cynthia* and at any rate
the earlier part of *Caliban.* The greater part of what W. L.
George wrote was shoddy rubbish, but in this particular book,
based on the career of Northcliffe, he achieved some memorable and truthful pictures of lower-middle class London life.
Parts of this book are probably autobiographical, and one of
the advantages of good bad writers is their lack of shame in
writing autobiography. Exhibitionism and self-pity are the
bane of the novelist, and yet if he is too frightened of them his
creative gift may suffer.

The existence of good bad literature—the fact that one can

be amused or excited or even moved by a book that one's intellect simply refuses to take seriously—is a reminder that art is not the same thing as cerebration. I imagine that by any test that could be devised, Carlyle would be found to be a more intelligent man than Trollope. Yet Trollope has remained readable and Carlyle has not: with all his cleverness he had not even the wit to write in plain straightforward English. In novelists, almost as much as in poets, the connection between intelligence and creative power is hard to establish. A good novelist may be a prodigy of self-discipline like Flaubert, or he may be an intellectual sprawl like Dickens. Enough talent to set up dozens of ordinary writers has been poured into Wyndham Lewis's so-called novels, such as *Tarr* or *Snooty Baronet*. Yet it would be a very heavy labor to read one of these books right through. Some indefinable quality, a sort of literary vitamin, which exists even in a book like *If Winter Comes*, is absent from them.

Perhaps the supreme example of the "good bad" book is *Uncle Tom's Cabin*. It is an unintentionally ludicrous book, full of preposterous melodramatic incidents; it is also deeply moving and essentially true; it is hard to say which quality outweighs the other. But *Uncle Tom's Cabin*, after all, is trying to be serious and to deal with the real world. How about the frankly escapist writers, the purveyors of thrills and "light" humor? How about *Sherlock Holmes, Vice Versa, Dracula, Helen's Babies* or *King Solomon's Mines*? All of these are definitely absurd books, books which one is more inclined to laugh *at* than *with*, and which were hardly taken seriously even by their authors; yet they have survived, and will probably continue to do so. All one can say is that, while civilization remains such that one needs distraction from time to time, "light" literature has its appointed place; also that there is such a thing as sheer skill, or native grace, which may have

more survival value than erudition or intellectual power.
There are music-hall songs which are better poems than three-
quarters of the stuff that gets into the anthologies:

> Come where the booze is cheaper,
> Come where the pots hold more,
> Come where the boss is a bit of a sport,
> Come to the pub next door!

Or again:

> Two lovely black eyes—
> Oh, what a surprise!
> Only for calling another man wrong,
> Two lovely black eyes!

I would far rather have written either of those than, say, *The
Blessed Damozel* or *Love in a Valley*. And by the same token
I would back *Uncle Tom's Cabin* to outlive the complete
works of Virginia Woolf or George Moore, though I know of
no strictly literary test which would show where the supe-
riority lies.

Nonsense Poetry

IN MANY LANGUAGES, IT IS SAID, THERE IS NO NONSENSE POETRY, and there is not a great deal of it even in English. The bulk of it is in nursery rhymes and scraps of folk poetry, some of which may not have been strictly nonsensical at the start, but have become so because their original application has been forgotten. For example, the rhyme about Margery Daw.

> See-saw, Margery Daw,
> Dobbin shall have a new master.
> He shall have but a penny a day
> Because he can't go any faster.

Or the other version that I learned in Oxfordshire as a little boy:

> See-saw, Margery Daw,
> Sold her bed and lay upon straw.
> Wasn't she a silly slut
> To sell her bed and lie upon dirt?

It may be that there was once a real person called Margery Daw, and perhaps there was even a Dobbin who somehow came into the story. When Shakespeare makes Edgar in *King Lear* quote "Pillicock sat on Pillicock hill," and similar fragments, he is uttering nonsense, but no doubt these fragments come from forgotten ballads in which they once had a meaning. The typical scrap of folk poetry which one quotes almost unconsciously is not exactly nonsense but a sort of musical

comment on some recurring event, such as "One a penny, two
a penny, Hot-Cross buns," or "Polly, put the kettle on, we'll
all have tea." Some of these seemingly frivolous rhymes actually express a deeply pessimistic view of life, the churchyard
wisdom of the peasant. For instance:

> Solomon Grundy,
> Born on Monday,
> Christened on Tuesday,
> Married on Wednesday,
> Took ill on Thursday,
> Worse on Friday,
> Died on Saturday,
> Buried on Sunday,
> And that was the end of Solomon Grundy

which is a gloomy story, but remarkably similar to yours or
mine.

Until Surrealism made a deliberate raid on the unconscious,
poetry that aimed at being nonsense, apart from the meaningless refrains of songs, does not seem to have been common.
This gives a special position to Edward Lear, whose nonsense
rhymes [1] have just been edited by Mr. R. L. Megroz, who was
also responsible for the Penguin edition a year or two before
the war. Lear was one of the first writers to deal in pure fantasy, with imaginary countries and made-up words, without
any satirical purpose. His poems are not all of them equally
nonsensical; some of them get their effect by a perversion of
logic, but they are all alike in that their underlying feeling is
sad and not bitter. They express a kind of amiable lunacy, a
natural sympathy with whatever is weak and absurd. Lear
could fairly be called the originator of the Limerick, though
verses in almost the same metrical form are to be found in
earlier writers, and what is sometimes considered a weakness

1 *The Lear Omnibus*. Edited by R. L. Megroz.

in his Limericks—that is, the fact that the rhyme is the same
in the first and last lines—is part of their charm. The very
slight change increases the impression of ineffectuality, which
might be spoiled if there were some striking surprise. For
example:

> There was a young lady of Portugal!
> Whose ideas were excessively nautical;
> She climbed up a tree
> To examine the sea,
> But declared she would never leave Portugal.

It is significant that almost no Limericks since Lear's have
been both printable and funny enough to seem worth quoting. But he is really seen at his best in certain longer poems,
such as "The Owl and the Pussy-cat" or "The Courtship of
the Yonghy-Bonghy-Bo":

> On the Coast of Coromandel,
> Where the early pumpkins blow,
> In the middle of the woods
> Lived the Yonghy-Bonghy-Bo.
> Two old chairs, and half a candle—
> One old pug without a handle—
> These were all his worldly goods:
> In the middle of the woods,
> These were all the worldly goods
> Of the Yonghy-Bonghy-Bo,
> Of the Yonghy-Bonghy-Bo.

Later there appears a lady with some white Dorking hens, and
an inconclusive love affair follows. Mr. Megroz thinks, plau-
sibly enough, that this may refer to some incident in Lear's
own life. He never married, and it is easy to guess that there
was something seriously wrong in his sex life. A psychiatrist
could no doubt find all kinds of significances in his drawings
and in the recurrence of certain made-up words such as

"runcible." His health was bad, and as he was the youngest
of twenty-one children in a poor family, he must have known
anxiety and hardship in very early life. It is clear that he was
unhappy and by nature solitary, in spite of having good
friends.

Aldous Huxley, in praising Lear's fantasies as a sort of
assertion of freedom, has pointed out that the "They" of the
Limericks represent common sense, legality and the duller
virtues generally. "They" are the realists, the practical men,
the sober citizens in bowler hats who are always anxious to
stop you doing anything worth doing. For instance:

> There was an old man of Whitehaven,
> Who danced a quadrille with a raven:
> But they said, "It's absurd
> To encourage this bird!"
> So they smashed that Old Man of Whitehaven.

To smash somebody just for dancing a quadrille with a raven
is exactly the kind of thing that "They" would do. Herbert
Read has also praised Lear, and is inclined to prefer his verse
to that of Lewis Carroll, as being purer fantasy. For myself,
I must say that I find Lear funniest when he is least arbitrary
and when a touch of burlesque or perverted logic makes its
appearance. When he gives his fancy free play, as in his imaginary names, or in things like "Three Receipts for Domestic
Cookery," he can be silly and tiresome. "The Pobble who has
no Toes" is haunted by the ghost of logic, and I think it is
the element of sense in it that makes it funny. The Pobble,
it may be remembered, went fishing in the Bristol Channel:

> And all the sailors and Admirals cried,
> When they saw him nearing the further side—
> "He has gone to fish, for his Aunt Jobiska's
> Runcible Cat with crimson whiskers!"

The thing that is funny here is the burlesque touch, the Admirals. What is arbitrary—the word "runcible," and the cat's crimson whiskers—is merely rather embarrassing. While the Pobble was in the water some unidentified creatures came and ate his toes off, and when he got home his aunt remarked:

> "It's a fact the whole world knows,
> That Pobbles are happier without their toes,"

which once again is funny because it has a meaning, and one might even say a political significance. For the whole theory of authoritarian government is summed up in the statement that Pobbles were happier without their toes. So also with the well-known Limerick:

> There was an Old Person of Basing,
> Whose presence of mind was amazing;
> He purchased a steed,
> Which he rode at full speed,
> And escaped from the people of Basing.

It is not quite arbitrary. The funniness is in the gentle implied criticism of the people of Basing, who once again are "They," the respectable ones, the right-thinking, art-hating majority.

The writer closest to Lear among his contemporaries was Lewis Carroll, who, however, was less essentially fantastic—and, in my opinion, funnier. Since then, as Mr. Megroz points out in his Introduction, Lear's influence has been considerable, but it is hard to believe that it has been altogether good. The silly whimsiness of present-day children's books could perhaps be partly traced back to him. At any rate, the idea of deliberately setting out to write nonsense, though it came off in Lear's case, is a doubtful one. Probably the best nonsense poetry is produced gradually and accidentally, by communities rather than by individuals. As a comic draughtsman, on the other hand, Lear's influence must have been beneficial. James Thurber, for instance, must surely owe something to Lear, directly or indirectly. With large numbers of Lear's own illustrations, and an informative Introduction, this book should make a first-rate Christmas present.

Riding Down from Bangor

THE REAPPEARANCE OF "HELEN'S BABIES," [1] IN ITS DAY ONE OF the most popular books in the world—within the British Empire alone it was pirated by twenty different publishing firms, the author receiving a total profit of £40 from a sale of some hundreds of thousands or millions of copies—will ring a bell in any literate person over thirty-five. Not that the present edition is an altogether satisfactory one. It is a cheap little book with rather unsuitable illustrations, various American dialect words appear to have been cut out of it, and the sequel, *Other People's Children*, which was often bound up with it in earlier editions, is missing. Still, it is pleasant to see *Helen's Babies* in print again. It had become almost a rarity in recent years, and it is one of the best of the little library of American books on which people born at about the turn of the century were brought up.

The books one reads in childhood, and perhaps most of all the bad and good bad books, create in one's mind a sort of false map of the world, a series of fabulous countries into which one can retreat at odd moments throughout the rest of life, and which in some cases can even survive a visit to the real countries which they are supposed to represent. The pampas, the Amazon, the coral islands of the Pacific, Russia, land of birch-tree and samovar, Transylvania with its boyars

[1] *Helen's Babies*. By John Habberton.

and vampires, the China of Guy Boothby, the Paris of du Maurier—one could continue the list for a long time. But one other imaginary country that I acquired early in life was called America. If I pause on the word "America," and, deliberately putting aside the existing reality, call up my childhood vision of it, I see two pictures—composite pictures, of course, from which I am omitting a good deal of the detail.

One is of a boy sitting in a whitewashed stone schoolroom. He wears braces and has patches on his shirt, and if it is summer he is barefooted. In the corner of the schoolroom there is a bucket of drinking water with a dipper. The boy lives in a farmhouse, also of stone and also whitewashed, which has a mortgage on it. He aspires to be President, and is expected to keep the woodbox full. Somewhere in the background of the picture, but completely dominating it, is a huge black Bible. The other picture is of a tall, angular man, with a shapeless hat pulled down over his eyes, leaning against a wooden paling and whittling at a stick. His lower jaw moves slowly but ceaselessly. At very long intervals he emits some piece of wisdom such as "A woman is the orneriest critter there is, 'ceptin' a mule," or "When you don't know a thing to do, don't do a thing"; but more often it is a jet of tobacco juice that issues from the gap in his front teeth. Between them those two pictures summed up my earliest impression of America. And of the two, the first—which, I suppose, represented New England, the other representing the South—had the stronger hold upon me.

The books from which these pictures were derived included, of course, books which it is still possible to take seriously, such as *Tom Sawyer* and *Uncle Tom's Cabin*, but the most richly American flavor was to be found in minor works which are now almost forgotten. I wonder, for instance, if anyone still reads *Rebecca of Sunnybrook Farm*, which remained a

popular favorite long enough to be filmed with Mary Pick-
ford in the leading part. Or how about the "Katy" books by
Susan Cooleridge (*What Katy Did at School,* etc.), which,
although girls' books and therefore "soppy," had the fascination of foreignness? Louisa M. Alcott's *Little Women* and
Good Wives are, I suppose, still flickeringly in print, and certainly they still have their devotees. As a child I loved both
of them, though I was less pleased by the third of the trilogy,
Little Men. That model school where the worst punishment
was to have to whack the schoolmaster, on "this hurts me
more than it hurts you" principles, was rather difficult to
swallow.

Helen's Babies belonged in much the same world as *Little
Women,* and must have been published round about the same
date. Then there were Artemus Ward, Bret Harte, and
various songs, hymns and ballads, besides poems dealing with
the Civil War, such as *Barbara Frietchie* (" 'Shoot if you must
this old grey head, But spare your country's flag,' she said")
and *Little Gifford of Tennessee.* There were other books so
obscure that it hardly seems worth mentioning them, and
magazine stories of which I remember nothing except that the
old homestead always seemed to have a mortgage on it. There
was also *Beautiful Joe,* the American reply to *Black Beauty,*
of which you might just possibly pick up a copy in a sixpenny
box. All the books I have mentioned were written well before
1900, but something of the special American flavor lingered on
into this century in, for instance, the Buster Brown colored
supplements, and even in Booth Tarkington's "Penrod"
stories, which will have been written round about 1910. Perhaps there was even a tinge of it in Ernest Thompson Seton's
animal books (*Wild Animals I Have Known,* etc.), which have
now fallen from favor but which drew tears from the pre-1914

child as surely as *Misunderstood* had done from the children of a generation earlier.

Somewhat later my picture of nineteenth-century America was given greater precision by a song which is still fairly well known and which can be found (I think) in the *Scottish Student's Song Book*. As usual in these bookless days I cannot get hold of a copy, and I must quote fragments from memory. It begins:

> Riding down from Bangor
> On an Eastern train,
> Bronzed with weeks of hunting
> In the woods of Maine—
> Quite extensive whiskers,
> Beard, moustache as well—
> Sat a student fellow,
> Tall and slim and swell.

Presently an aged couple and a "village maiden," described as "beautiful, petite," get into the carriage. Quantities of cinders are flying about, and before long the student fellow gets one in his eye: the village maiden extracts it for him, to the scandal of the aged couple. Soon after this the train shoots into a long tunnel, "black as Egypt's night." When it emerges into the daylight again the maiden is covered with blushes, and the cause of her confusion is revealed when—

> There suddenly appeared
> A tiny little ear-ring
> In that horrid student's beard!

I do not know the date of the song, but the primitiveness of the train (no lights in the carriage, and a cinder in one's eye a normal accident) suggests that it belongs well back in the nineteenth century.

What connects this song with books like *Helen's Babies* is first of all a sort of sweet innocence—the climax, the thing you are supposed to be slightly shocked at, is an episode with which any modern piece of naughty-naughty would *start*—and, secondly, a faint vulgarity of language mixed up with a certain cultural pretentiousness. *Helen's Babies* is intended as a humorous, even a farcical book, but it is haunted all the way through by words like "tasteful" and "ladylike," and it is funny chiefly because its tiny disasters happen against a background of conscious gentility. "Handsome, intelligent, composed, tastefully dressed, without a suspicion of the flirt or the languid woman of fashion about her, she awakened to the utmost my every admiring sentiment"—thus is the heroine described, figuring elsewhere as "erect, fresh, neat, composed, bright-eyed, fair-faced, smiling and observant." One gets beautiful glimpses of a now-vanished world in such remarks as: "I believe you arranged the floral decorations at St. Zephaniah's Fair last winter, Mr. Burton? 'Twas the most tasteful display of the season." But in spite of the occasional use of " 'twas," and other archaisms—"parlor" for sitting-room, "chamber" for bedroom, "real" as an adverb, and so forth—the book does not "date" very markedly, and many of its admirers imagine it to have been written round about 1900. Actually it was written in 1875, a fact which one might infer from internal evidence, since the hero, aged twenty-eight, is a veteran of the Civil War.

The book is very short and the story is a simple one. A young bachelor is prevailed on by his sister to look after her house and her two sons, aged five and three, while she and her husband go on a fortnight's holiday. The children drive him almost mad by an endless succession of such acts as falling into ponds, swallowing poison, throwing keys down wells, cutting themselves with razors, and the like, but also facilitate his engagement to "a charming girl whom, for about a year, I had been adoring from afar." These events take place in an outer suburb of New York, in a society which now seems astonishingly sedate, formal, domesticated and, according to current conceptions, un-American. Every action is governed by etiquette. To pass a carriage full of ladies when your hat is crooked is an ordeal; to recognize an acquaintance in church is ill-bred; to become engaged after a ten-days' courtship is a severe social lapse. We are accustomed to thinking of American society as more crude, adventurous and, in a cultural sense, democratic than our own, and from writers like Mark Twain, Whitman and Bret Harte, not to mention the cowboy and Red Indian stories of the weekly papers, one draws a picture of a wild anarchic world peopled by eccentrics and desperadoes who have no traditions and no attachment to one place. That aspect of nineteenth-century America did of course exist, but in the more populous eastern States a society similar to Jane Austen's seems to have survived longer than it did in England. And it is hard not to feel that it was a better kind of society than that which arose from the sudden industrialization of the later part of the century. The people in *Helen's Babies* or *Little Women* may be mildly ridiculous, but they are uncorrupted. They have something that is perhaps best described as integrity, or good morale, founded partly on an unthinking piety. It is a matter of course that everyone attends church on Sunday morning and says grace before meals and prayers at bedtime: to amuse the children one tells them Bible stories, and if they ask for a song it is probably "Glory, glory Hallelujah." Perhaps it is also a sign of spiritual health in the "light" literature of this period that death is mentioned freely. "Baby Phil," the brother of Budge and Toddie, has died shortly before *Helen's Babies* opens, and there are various tear-jerking references to his "tiny coffin." A modern writer attempting a story of this kind would have kept coffins out of it.

English children are still Americanized by way of the films, but it would no longer be generally claimed that American books are the best ones for children. Who, without misgivings, would bring up a child on the colored "comics" in which sinister professors manufacture atomic bombs in underground laboratories while Superman whizzes through the clouds, the machine-gun bullets bouncing off his chest like peas, and platinum blondes are raped, or very nearly, by steel robots and fifty-foot dinosaurs? It is a far cry from Superman to the Bible and the woodpile. The earlier children's books, or books readable by children, had not only innocence but a sort of native gaiety, a buoyant, carefree feeling, which was the product, presumably, of the un-heard-of freedom and security which nineteenth-century America enjoyed. That is the connecting link between books so seemingly far apart as *Little Women* and *Life on the Mississippi*. The society described in the one is subdued, bookish and home-loving, while the other tells of a crazy world of bandits, gold mines, duels, drunkenness and gambling hells: but in both one can detect an underlying confidence in the future, a sense of freedom and opportunity.

Nineteenth-century America was a rich, empty country which lay outside the main stream of world events, and in which the twin nightmares that beset nearly every modern man, the nightmare of unemployment and the nightmare of State interference, had hardly come into being. There were social distinctions, more marked than those of today, and there was poverty (in *Little Women*, it will be remembered, the family is at one time so hard up that one of the girls sells her hair to the barber), but there was not, as there is now, an all-prevailing sense of helplessness. There was room for everybody, and if you worked hard you could be certain of a living—could even be certain of growing rich: this was generally believed, and for the greater part of the population it was even broadly true. In other words, the civilization of nineteenth-century America was capitalist civilization at its best. Soon after the Civil War the inevitable deterioration started. But for some decades, at least, life in America was much better fun than life in Europe—there was more happening, more color, more variety, more opportunity—and the books and songs of that period had a sort of bloom, a childlike quality. Hence, I think, the popularity of *Helen's Babies* and other "light" literature, which made it normal for the English child of thirty or forty years ago to grow up with a theoretical knowledge of raccoons, woodchucks, chipmunks, gophers, hickory trees, watermelons and other unfamiliar fragments of the American scene.